'Shall we [...]
ourselves m[...]
suggested sof[...]

A tense silence twisted between them.

Libby hesitated, torn between the weight of her desire and the ignobility of inviting a man into her bed who had no regard for her, thought she was nothing but a gold-digger.

She shivered violently and Marc pulled the robe closer around her. 'Let me help you out of those wet things,' he murmured playfully, and leaned closer to kiss her again.

Libby kissed him back tentatively, and suddenly the caress deepened, sensuality heightened and she forgot her misgivings... forgot everything except the raw primal need that was racing between them.

'OK, you can take me to bed.' She whispered the words against his lips. 'Just this once...but it doesn't mean anything...'

Even as she spoke he was swinging her up into his arms.

Kathryn Ross was born in Zambia, where her parents happened to live at that time. Educated in Ireland and England, she now lives in a village near Blackpool, Lancashire. Kathryn is a professional beauty therapist, but writing is her first love. As a child she wrote adventure stories, and at thirteen was editor of her school magazine. Happily, ten writing years later, DESIGNED WITH LOVE was accepted by Mills & Boon®. A romantic Sagittarian, she loves travelling to exotic locations.

Recent titles by the same author:

THE MILLIONAIRE'S SECRET MISTRESS
A LATIN PASSION
THE FRENCHMAN'S MISTRESS
A SPANISH ENGAGEMENT

MISTRESS TO A RICH MAN

BY
KATHRYN ROSS

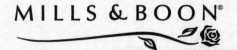

MILLS & BOON®

First published in Great Britain 2005
Harlequin Mills & Boon Limited,
Eton House, 18-24 Paradise Road, Richmond, Surrey TW9 1SR

© Kathryn Ross 2005

ISBN 0 263 84205 3

Set in Times Roman 10½ on 12 pt.
01-1205-52318

Printed and bound in Spain
by Litografia Rosés, S.A., Barcelona

CHAPTER ONE

THEY said that the female of the species was usually deadlier than the male. Libby didn't exactly hold with that theory, not after Simon had, a) not only put her bank balance in the red, but b) also succeeded in breaking her heart.

How he had managed to do the latter, she wasn't sure. All she knew was that you didn't instantly stop loving someone just because they said one morning over breakfast, 'Sorry this isn't working out,' before casually picking up an already packed holdall from the hall cupboard.

All right, the way he had finished with her had been callously sudden and there had been times during their relationship when he had been a little bit on the selfish side. But there had also been wonderful times and unfortunately these were the memories that plagued her sometimes late into the night. Why was the brain so stupidly selective? Why couldn't she just remember the bad times, or at least concentrate on the fact that because of Simon she was going to have to move out of her apartment, as, despite the fact that she had a good job in advertising, her bills had mounted up to the point where she couldn't afford to live in Merrion Terrace on her own.

And now to add insult to injury it seemed that Simon had run up another set of huge bills on her credit card.

'It was my card but a joint account,' Libby confided to her best friend Chloe as they met for their usual Friday drink in the wine bar after work. 'I suppose I should have cancelled it when he left, but I honestly never thought he'd do anything like this.'

'Have you talked to him about it?'

'Not yet.' Libby took a sip of her wine, her expression grim. 'He's not answering his mobile. But I'm having some time off work next week to go flat-hunting, so I'll try and track him down then.'

Although it was only five-thirty the bar was filling up as business people from the surrounding offices piled in for a swift drink before heading home. By eight the place would be deserted again; it was the same every Friday in this part of London.

Chloe leaned forward suddenly. 'Don't look now, but there's a man watching you from the next table. And he keeps leaning over as if he's trying to listen to what you are saying.'

'I'm not interested, Chloe. To be honest, the way I feel right now I think I am off men for life.' Libby didn't even bother to glance around.

'Nonsense. You'll meet somebody else and fall madly in love.'

'I don't even know if I believe in love any more.' Libby finished her wine and put the glass down firmly on the table. 'I really don't think I'd trust my heart to someone else again. In fact, next time…if there is a next time…I'm going to be ruled by my head—go for someone with loads of money.'

Although the words were said with firm resolution, Chloe wasn't convinced for one moment. She glanced over at her friend and laughed. 'Yeah, right, and this from the girl who would lend you her last penny and forget to ask for it back.'

'Well, this is the new me,' Libby said resolutely. 'Would you like another drink?' As Libby glanced to-

wards the bar her eyes caught the giant TV screen behind
it. The news was on and they were showing pictures of a
man getting out of a stretched limousine. As the camera
zoomed in on him Libby felt her breath freeze in her
throat…felt the crowds in the bar melt away.

It was Carl Sheridan…*her father!* But how could it be?
Confusion and shock vied for position inside her. Her father was dead…her mother had told her so years ago.

She stared at the screen doubting her own eyes for a
moment, but even though she had only been seven years
of age the last time she'd seen him she knew it was her
father. He hadn't changed that much, same jet-dark hair
and piercing blue eyes that Libby had inherited. What was
her father doing on television? And where had he been
for all these long years? And, more importantly, why had
her mother told her he was dead?

'Libby, are you all right?' Chloe's voice seemed to be
coming from a long way away.

'Not really…no.' Libby shook her head and couldn't
drag her eyes away from the TV. 'That's my dad!'

'Who?' Chloe followed her gaze.

'That man… Carl Sheridan… What are they saying
about him?' Libby strained her ears, but it was impossible
to hear what was being said on the TV over the noise in
the bar.

'That's Carl Quinton… He's an American movie star,
Libby.' Chloe shook her head in puzzlement.

Libby looked back at her friend in surprise. Chloe
worked in PR and she followed the media pages very
closely. Usually she was spot on, knew exactly who was
who. But this time she had got it wrong. 'I'm telling you,
Chloe, he's my dad and he is not an American, he's a
Londoner.'

Chloe frowned. 'Well, he is known as Carl Quinton

now, Libby. I was reading an article about him just the other day.'

'And what did the article say?' Libby asked numbly.

'It said he started out in a made-for-TV drama for a local network in California and everyone loved him. Then he was offered a starring role on Broadway. And since then he's been a big hit in the States, but maybe not too well known in Europe yet. However, all that is set to change because he's really hit the big time now and is co-starring with Julia Hynes in a film called *Family Values*, which is about to première in Cannes.'

What Chloe was telling her was so completely mind-blowing that Libby couldn't quite take it in. 'Are you sure we are talking about the same person?'

'Absolutely. He's quite a personality in the States, lives in Beverly Hills and he's been married and divorced three times. There was no mention of any children, though.'

'Well, whether he mentioned them or not I am his daughter,' Libby said softly. 'And his real name is Carl Sheridan.' She transferred her attention back to the TV where he was still talking to a reporter. 'He and my mother split up when I was seven.'

'Excuse me.' The man at the next table pulled at the sleeve of Libby's jacket. 'Did I hear you say that Carl Quinton is your father?' Libby glanced around at the man; he was about her age, twenty-seven, and had thick blond hair, a pale face and sharply inquisitive grey eyes. There was something about the way he asked the question that was very unsettling.

'No.' Libby shrugged away from his hand.

But, not to be thwarted, the man moved to sit on the vacant stool at their table. 'My name is John Wright and I'm a freelance journalist. I'd be very interested to hear the inside story of Carl Quinton's life.'

'I don't know the inside story of Carl Quinton's life.'

'I take it you haven't seen your father for a while?' Although his tone was friendly, his manner was very insistent.

'Please go away and mind your own business,' Libby snapped.

'Look, I couldn't help overhearing that you are a bit strapped for cash at the moment. I'll pay you for the story,' the man continued briskly. 'And pay you very well—'

'I don't want your money.' Libby stood up. 'Chloe, I've got to get out of here.'

Libby couldn't remember leaving the bar. But it was a relief to be outside even though the rain was bouncing off the London streets.

They were both soaked through by the time they flagged down a taxi and climbed in. 'What did that man give you?' Chloe asked.

'He didn't give me anything.'

'Yes, he did.' Chloe leaned over and tapped her hand.

Libby uncurled her fist and was surprised to see a card there. It said 'John Wright Investigative Journalist' and there was a telephone number.

Libby scrunched the card up and shoved it in her pocket. 'All he wants is to rake through the mud.' And there was a surprising amount of mud to rake through as well, she thought angrily.

Leaning her head back against the seat of the taxi, she shut her eyes. She was shivering uncontrollably, but whether it was with cold or shock she wasn't sure.

Libby remembered how much she had loved her father; she also remembered the close bond they had once shared. Even now she could remember the way he had lifted her up in his arms, teasing her and flying her through the air making her giggle uncontrollably. And how some nights he had been the one to tuck her up in bed, read her a story and kiss her goodnight; she could still remember the scent of his cologne. But her most poignant memory was the day he had left.

'I have to leave, sweetheart, but it doesn't mean I don't love you.'

She remembered begging him not to go, tears rolling down her face.

'I have to, sweetheart. But I'll come back.'

She tried to hold onto him, but her mother pulled her away.

'Daddy...please...please...' She struggled and escaped to run after him, but reached the door just as he closed it behind him.

Even remembering that moment now upset her. Her father had never returned. And she hadn't heard anything from him since that day. Every birthday and every Christmas she had waited for some contact from him, but none had ever been made.

Then just before her tenth birthday her mother had gently pulled her to one side and told her he was dead. *Why had she done that?* The frustrating thing was that Libby could no longer ask her mother, as she and her stepfather had died in a train crash twelve months ago.

Up until now she had thought she had no family left.

'What will you do now?' Chloe asked curiously.

Libby opened her eyes. 'I'm going to find him, of course.' Her voice was filled with husky determination. 'I need answers to questions. I need to see him.'

CHAPTER TWO

THE South of France sparkled in the afternoon sun and as the plane turned and banked ready for landing Libby had a perfect view over thickly wooded hills and a bay where millionaires' yachts bobbled peacefully on turquoise water. As they came even lower she could see Nice shimmering on the Bay of Angels. Despite the fact that she was feeling apprehensive about the prospect of seeing her father again after all this time, Libby felt a burst of happiness. It was hard not to feel good when the sky was so clear and the sea so blue. Everything would work out, she told herself firmly. Her father would meet her while she was here and… And what? she thought in sudden panic. All the pain of losing him for twenty years would disappear? It was unrealistic to expect that. She was just going to have to take this a day at a time and not expect anything too much. For all she knew her father might not even turn up, might not want to see her.

Getting in contact with him had been harder than she had thought. First she had tried to get in touch with him through his film studio in California, but one person after another had given her the run-around on the phone and she could tell that they didn't believe she was Carl Quinton's daughter, but just thought she was some crazed fan. So in the end she'd had to use Chloe's contacts in the PR world to find out who her father's agent was so she could contact her dad through him.

She had been a bit surprised to learn that his agent was Marc Clayton, one of the most powerful and influential

moguls in the business. Her father really had hit the big
time to have Marc Clayton batting in his corner because
anybody who was anybody wanted to be represented by
him and he could pick and choose from the cream of
celebrity lists. He had the reputation of being a ruthless
businessman, but he always got the best deals for his clients, his company handled all their publicity, and in the
process he created megastars. He had also made himself
a millionaire by the age of thirty-three and was something
of a celebrity himself.

Libby had seen him on TV at premières and she had
seen his picture in the paper. There had even been pictures
in glossy magazines of his wedding to the beautiful film
actress Marietta and more pictures when they'd had a
baby a few months later. But although they had seemed
to be the perfect golden couple the marriage hadn't
worked, and twelve months later they were divorced. No
reason had been given for the split and neither had married again. From what she could gather his ex was still
hotly pursuing her career in Hollywood, while Marc spent
more and more time in Europe where he had opened a
number of new offices.

When Libby had sent him an email with an attached
letter for her father she had expected to be given the same
run-around that the film company had given her. So she
had taken the initiative and booked herself a flight to the
South of France and a hotel room for seven nights. She
knew her father would be there for the Cannes film festival so if she couldn't contact him indirectly she would
track him down in person, even if it meant hanging around
outside the convention centre night and day.

There had been no reply to that first email so Libby
had sent a second telling Marc Clayton her plans and making it very clear that she would see her father with or

without his help. She had been surprised to receive an immediate response from him apologising for not getting back to her sooner.

He had told her that he had passed on her message and that her father was very much looking forward to seeing her in Cannes, but due to prior commitments would not be arriving in France until two days after her. However, in the meantime would she do him the honour of having dinner with him on the night of her arrival?

The plane touched down on the runway with a thud. She had to admit that not receiving a direct reply from her father had been disappointing. The dinner invitation from Marc Clayton had been a total surprise. Even now as she gathered her belongings she couldn't help but wonder why her father's agent would want to have dinner with her.

It didn't take long to collect her luggage and make her way through customs and out into the terminal.

Marc Clayton spotted her immediately. From the first moment her email had arrived on his desk he'd known she was going to be trouble. But when he saw her walk across the airport terminal he knew she was going to be double trouble. He had hired a private investigator to check her out, but the photo that had landed on his desk had certainly not done her justice. Libby Sheridan was quite stunning and there was no denying she was Carl's daughter; he could see the resemblance. Tall and leggy she walked with an air of graceful confidence across the concourse, long dark hair shimmering as shafts of sunlight caught its chestnut highlights. She wasn't exactly rake-thin, but her curves were in all the right places, and she wore cropped jeans and a pale blue T-shirt that emphasised her long waist and firm curves. Her only luggage was a soft canvas holdall that she carried over one shoulder.

She was making for the exit towards the bus stops when he called her.

'Ms Elizabeth Sheridan?'

She swung around, crystal-blue eyes wide and questioning. 'Yes?'

He watched as she walked a little closer, her manner wary.

'You sent me an email telling me you were coming. I'm Marc Clayton.' He extended a hand towards her.

'Oh!' It took her a moment to put down her bag and reach to shake his hand. 'I didn't expect to see you here.'

As her hand was taken in a firm grip and she looked up into the darkness of his eyes Libby's heartbeats started to increase dramatically. She knew from photographs that Marc Clayton was handsome, but she was totally unprepared for just *how* handsome he was in the flesh. The guy was drop dead gorgeous. There was something intensely sexy about the velvet darkness of his eyes and the way his thick dark hair was brushed back from a face that was hard-boned in structure with a strong square jaw. And he was tall...well over six feet with the body of an athlete, wide, powerful shoulders tapering to a flat stomach and lithe hips. But it was the air of power that seemed to permeate his every word, his every look, that was most unsettling.

'I thought as your father isn't here I should step into the breach and see you safely to your hotel.' Before she could stop him he reached and picked up her bag.

'Well, that is very kind. But it really isn't necessary.' Libby was slightly nonplussed. She knew very well how valuable this man's time was. Chloe had impressed that upon her before she had left. Apparently Chloe's boss had once tried to set up a meeting with him and been given a very polite but firm brush-off by his secretary. Marc

Clayton's diary was full, had been the message. In fact they had joked in Chloe's office that for the likes of their small firm Marc Clayton would probably be busy until the year two thousand and fifty. 'He's a very influential man, Libby,' Chloe had told her earnestly. 'Getting an appointment with him is like finding gold in the Thames.'

So what was he doing here, making time for her? The Cannes Film Festival was set to start soon, so the guy must have had a million more important places to be.

There wasn't time to ask because before she could say anything further he was leading the way outside, his pace brisk.

The heat of the afternoon was intense; it shimmered over the tarmac road and was so overwhelming that Libby felt herself flagging as she struggled to keep up with his long strides.

They reached a pale blue open-top Mercedes and Marc opened the boot and flung her case in. Then he took the jacket of his expensive sand-coloured suit off and slung that on the back seat before opening the passenger door for her.

'Now, I know you told me in your email that you had booked into the Rosette hotel, but when I checked it out I decided it really wasn't suitable so I hope you don't mind but I have taken the liberty of changing you to the Emporium hotel.' The words were so brisk and authoritative that it took Libby a moment to register the fact that, actually, no, it wasn't OK.

'Why did you do that?' She didn't get into the car.

'Because the Rosette is a two-star hotel and the Emporium a five-star, so naturally I thought you would be more comfortable in the latter.'

Libby felt a flare of anger. She had always been a very independent woman and she didn't like the feeling of being taken over like this. 'Mr Clayton, I booked the Rosette hotel because that was where I wanted to stay.' She refrained from saying that she had chosen her hotel because it suited her budget at the moment. A five-star hotel was certainly out of the question, especially as her ex still hadn't paid the money he had spent on her credit card.

Marc Clayton looked vaguely amused, as if he couldn't believe that anyone would want to stay in a two-star hotel, which made Libby's temper rise further. 'You know, Mr Clayton, I do appreciate the fact that you have come out of your way to pick me up today, but I can't help wondering why.'

'I told you why.' He shrugged. 'In your father's absence I thought I had better make sure you were OK.'

'I can assure you that I don't need looking after.' She tilted her chin up in a slightly stubborn kind of way and met his eyes determinedly. There was a part of her that was tempted to tell him angrily that her father hadn't looked after her since she was the age of seven so she certainly didn't need any man's help now. But she held her tongue on that because strangely it seemed like a betrayal to her father...although why she should feel such loyalty to him now she didn't know.

As Marc glanced down at her he noticed the brief flicker of vulnerability and sadness in the delicate blue beauty of her eyes. The look took him by surprise. Then she seemed to pull herself up and the fire of confident determination returned in her expression, making him wonder if he had in fact imagined the moment.

'Anyway, Mr Clayton, I would appreciate it if you would just drop me at the hotel that *I* booked. For one thing it suits my budget at the moment, and for another it is where I have told everyone I will be staying.'

'Ah...I see.' It hadn't taken her that long to get around

to mentioning money, Marc thought wryly. Now this was more what he had expected from her.

Libby was momentarily thrown by the meaningful tone of his voice. 'What do you see?'

'Do you want to get in?' He nodded towards the car. 'I shouldn't really be parked here so I'd like to move. We can talk as we go.'

'OK.' As she moved past him and into the passenger seat he had a good view of her very shapely rear. She was incredibly sexy…it was a distraction he didn't need.

The leather seat was hot beneath her skin, the sun pumping down from a clear blue sky. Libby rummaged in her handbag and found a rubber band, then pulled her hair up and away from her neck and secured it in a pony-tail.

'I didn't realise it was going to be as hot as this,' she murmured.

'This is the South of France.' Marc smiled wryly.

'Yes.' She shrugged. 'I know, but it is only May. And it's been so cold and miserable at home. When it's like that it's hard to believe that the sun is shining anywhere.' She turned her face up to the sky. 'This is wonderful…makes me wish I could stay longer than a week.'

'Well, the weather can be changeable here in May,' Marc told her hurriedly. 'We can get torrential rain and the mistral can blow.' He didn't want her hanging around too long! She could cause real havoc with his promotion plans for Carl's film!

Marc glanced around at her as he pulled the car out onto the main road. He could see the lovely shape of her face now, the high cheekbones, the slightly tip tilt of her small nose, and the smooth perfection of her skin. She looked like a teenager with her hair in that pony-tail, fresh and exciting and… Swiftly he changed the direction of

his thoughts away from such dangerous ground; if he carried on like that she could cause havoc to more than his
business plans. He tried to concentrate on the real reason
she was here.

'So I take it money is tight at the moment, otherwise
you'd be staying longer...and you'd be in a better hotel.'

Libby looked across at him, the impertinent question
taking her by surprise. 'I can't stay any longer because
I've got to go back to work soon. And I have chosen the
Rosette hotel because that is where I want to be, thank
you.'

'You mean it will do for now.'

The dry disbelief in his tone made her sit straighter in
her seat. 'Just what on earth are you getting at, Mr
Clayton?' Despite her best efforts her tone was very sharp.

'I'm trying to get to the truth, Ms Sheridan. Or shall I
call you Libby...that is what everyone calls you, isn't it?'

'That's what my friends call me.' Her tone dripped with
ice now.

He smiled at that. 'And you can call me Marc.' He
changed gear as he headed the car up towards the motor-
way. 'You see, I am a very busy man...*Libby*...'

She noticed how he leaned heavy emphasis on her
name.

'So I suggest we just cut to the bottom line.'

'And what would that be?' Libby asked, a small frown
playing between her eyebrows.

'How much do you want?'

The question meant nothing to Libby. Her frown deepened. 'Do you mind telling me what on earth you are
talking about?'

'I am talking about the fact that, despite your father's
best efforts, you have wanted nothing to do with him for
all these years.'

Libby was so shocked by the statement that she couldn't find her voice to answer. What best efforts? she wondered hazily. She hadn't heard a word from her father since the day he'd walked out...not one word!

'And now you know Carl has hit the big time, found fame and fortune, and suddenly you have arrived on his doorstep,' Marc continued on in a laconic tone and slanted a wry glance over at her. 'Call me cynical if you wish, Libby, but your timing leads me to believe that you have more than a quiet little family reunion in mind.'

'What I have in mind, Mr Clayton, is none of your damn business.' Libby's voice trembled with shock and with fury. 'How dare you suggest something so repugnant? You don't even know me...you know nothing of my relationship with my father.'

'Well, I know what your father has told me.'

Those words sent even deeper shock waves coursing through Libby. 'What has he told you?'

Marc glanced over at her again. He noted the wide horror in her eyes, the high spots of red colour in her cheeks. 'You know, you should think about taking up acting,' he said calmly. 'You are really quite good.'

'Maybe it runs in the family.' She muttered the words under her breath.

'Maybe it does.' He glanced around at her.

She shook her head. 'What did my father tell you?' The words felt like wood in her mouth. There was a part of her that didn't want to hear this. She felt sick inside. It was bad enough that she had grown up without at least hearing from her father, but that he should lie about the fact was very painful. *Why would he do that?*

'He told me that all through your life he has sent you cards and letters, money and expensive gifts, and that the cards and letters have always been returned but the gifts and the money were kept.'

'I don't believe he told you that.' Libby's voice was brittle. 'Why are you saying these things to me?'

'Because they are true, you know they are true. And then on your eighteenth birthday he tried to make direct contact with you. He turned up at your party and you slammed the door in his face. Told him you hated him and never wanted to see him again.'

Libby opened and closed her mouth. She wanted to tell him that it was all a damn lie, but calling her father a liar to this…appalling stranger was more than she could bear. 'This is none of your business,' she said instead, her voice trembling. 'I loved my father.'

'Loved?' Marc Clayton glanced around at her, one dark eyebrow raised wryly. 'That's past tense, isn't it?'

Libby swallowed hard. 'I still love him now.' It was hard to say the words, especially to Marc Clayton, but they were nonetheless true. No matter what, she did still love her father. And he must have had his reasons for doing what he had done…saying what he had said. She desperately wanted to believe that he had, which surprised her somewhat because up until now she hadn't realised just how much she wanted everything to be OK between her and her dad, wanted to fly into his arms and have that old bond back between them. She had missed him so much.

Libby averted her face from Marc Clayton as she felt tears welling up behind her eyes. She was damned if she would give this arrogant man the satisfaction of knowing he had got to her.

'Well, anyway, I think, putting all that aside, it would be best if we could come to some arrangement before the press start to poke their noses around in this,' Marc continued briskly.

'What kind of arrangement?' Libby asked angrily.

Marc pulled the car to a standstill at the tollbooth and threw some money into the machine. The tinkle of coins filled the silence between them. 'That kind of arrangement,' Marc said dryly.

'I don't want your flaming money.'

'Just your father's? Or maybe you think you can sell your story to the press and become the darling of the talk show circuits for a while?'

'Go to hell,' Libby said furiously.

'We need to sort things out—'

'Anything I have to sort out I will be sorting out with my father. Not you.'

'For a start, you can of course stay at the Emporium hotel and I will take care of the bill—'

'You are not listening to me.' Libby glared at him, her eyes overbright. 'This is between my father and I. And I will not be staying at the Emporium. If you take me there I will simply leave.'

'You are very stubborn, aren't you?' Marc replied tersely.

She said nothing to that.

'OK, have it your way. I'll drop you at the Rosette.'

Still she made no reply, but continued to stare out at the passing scenery.

They were travelling along the palm-lined Croisette now. In ordinary circumstances Libby would have been enjoying the drive, would have been drinking in the sights along the promenade, the designer shops and the beautiful architecture. There were large posters up everywhere promoting the films that were being shown here next week for the festival. One of them was her father's film. There was a giant picture of him and his co-star Julia Hynes next to the Carlton hotel with the words, 'Meet Jack Winger the guy who believes in FAMILY VALUES'. The poster appeared several times along the promenade. Her father looked incredibly handsome on it, much younger than his forty-five years. Libby could hardly believe that he was starring opposite such a big star as Julia Hynes.

'I take it Jack Winger is the character my father is playing in this film?' Libby asked, suddenly forgetting that she had decided she wasn't talking any more to Marc Clayton.

'Yes. And he's all set to be a tremendous box-office success. Your father is a brilliant actor.'

Marc turned the car away from the blue sparkle of the Mediterranean and the colourful awnings that lined the private beaches.

'I'm afraid your hotel is quite a long way back from the promenade,' Marc murmured.

Libby glanced over at him. 'Maybe, but I'm willing to bet it is not as far away from where my father is staying as the hotel you wanted to put me in.'

There was a gleam of amusement in Marc's dark eyes for a moment. 'You are very suspicious, do you know that?'

She slanted him a wry look. 'And you're not?'

His lips twisted in an amused smile. '*Touché.*'

'So where is my father staying when he finally arrives?'

When there was no immediate response Libby shook her head. 'Well, I'll hazard a guess that it's the Carlton, shall I? From what I can remember about my father he always did like the best of places.'

'Was that where you were holding out for…an all-expenses-paid stay at the Carlton hotel?'

Libby's lips twisted in dry distaste. 'But of course,' she

murmured flippantly. 'And naturally I would only have accepted a suite with a balcony and sea view.' She was joking, but one glance at Marc Clayton and she knew he thought she was serious. Anger bubbled through her. This guy really was a piece of work. Arrogant...insufferable and with an opinion of her that was obviously lower than low. Well, what did she care? she asked herself swiftly. He was nothing to her. So what if he wanted to think of her as a gold-digging menace? She would let him get on with it, just as long as he didn't get in the way of her reunion with her father...or, worse, influence her father's thoughts!

'My father does know I'm here, doesn't he?' she asked suddenly.

'Yes, I told you. I passed on your email.'

'Right.' Libby bit down on her lip. 'Do you think he got it?'

Marc pulled the car up outside a small hotel. 'Yes, he definitely got it.'

He switched the engine off and then looked across at her. 'Your father and I have become good friends over the last couple of years. I certainly wouldn't keep anything from him...especially something I know means so much to him.'

'You think I mean a lot to him?' The husky question was out before she could help it.

For a second Marc glimpsed again that vulnerable look about her, the flicker of deep sadness in her blue eyes. And it had a strange effect on him; it made him want to reach out and touch her, draw her close, hold her... He frowned to himself. She was a cold-blooded gold-digger and a damn good actress, he reminded himself.

'You know you mean a lot to him. He was devastated when he lost you.' Marc said the words firmly. 'I've sat with him while he has poured his heart out about the day when he last held his daughter. Believe me, every day he has spent apart from you has been a wrench for him.'

Libby stared up at him, her heart beating so fiercely against her chest that it hurt. She wanted to believe that so much...

Marc watched the expression in her beautiful blue eyes and impulsively he reached out and touched the side of her face. 'It will be OK.' Even as he said the words he was wondering why he felt he should comfort her. It was as if some sort of spell were weaving its way between them.

Libby felt it too, and the touch of his hand against her skin sent some very unexpected emotions racing through her. One moment she was thinking about her father and the next she was looking up into Marc Clayton's dark eyes and it was as if she were drowning and spinning in a coil of sexual tension that came completely out of nowhere.

Confusion and desire mixed inside her, a heady, lethal concoction that fought one against the other, making her heart race even harder. She noticed his gaze moving towards the softness of her lips and she moistened them nervously.

What would it be like to be kissed by Marc Clayton?

The question shocked her. You don't even like him, she told herself fiercely. He's arrogant and insulting.

Even so it took all of Libby's self-control to pull away from him, back from the brink of disaster. This man was playing games with her, she told herself angrily. He was saying something nice and acting in a sympathetic manner because for some reason he wanted to control the situation.

'Of course I'll be OK,' she said, and from somewhere she summoned up a brisk confidence she was far from feeling. 'And I'll be even more OK after I have met up with my father.'

'I'm sure he will see you right financially, if that's what you mean.' Marc's lips twisted wryly. 'You know, for just a second there that little-girl-lost look of yours was very convincing. I could almost...*almost*...believe that you genuinely cared about your father.'

Libby's blue eyes narrowed on him. And to think that two seconds ago she had been wondering what it would be like to kiss him; she must have been out of her tiny mind! 'Well, that makes two of us, because for almost a minute there I could almost believe that you were a caring human being.'

Marc watched as she stepped out of the car onto the pavement and a small smile curved his lips. He hated to admit it, but there was something about her fiery confidence that he admired. OK, he was too much of a hard-headed businessman to be taken in by her, but she did intrigue him.

Libby went around to the back of the vehicle, intending to take her bag and leave him without another word, but unfortunately she couldn't open the boot of the car.

'Need some help?' Marc climbed out from behind the driving wheel and smirked. She made no reply, just stepped back and watched as he retrieved her bag for her.

'Thank you.' She held out her hand for her luggage, but he didn't pass it across for her.

'I'll carry it inside for you.'

'There's really no need—'

'Oh I think there is every need,' he said calmly. 'After all, I have promised your father that I will look after you. So I can't just leave you, can I?'

'I wish you would,' Libby grated under her breath.

But Marc didn't hear her; he was already heading off into the hotel without her.

'Look, I will be fine now,' she murmured as she followed him into the reception.

Marc didn't say anything, just rang the bell on the reception desk. Libby fell silent as they waited for someone to arrive. There was no point telling Marc to go again; he was obviously just going to do as he damn well pleased. He was *so* annoying.

In order to keep her mind off just how annoying he was, she glanced around at her surroundings. There was a lounge at the other end of the reception with several settees and chairs. The place was a bit dark, but the décor was stylish and it looked clean. There were some lilies on the desk and their sweet scent permeated the air.

'The place looks OK,' Marc said as her gaze returned to him.

'I knew it would be,' she lied with a shrug. In fact she had just hoped for the best when she'd made the reservation.

A man came out from the back and Marc started to talk to him in fluent French. This threw Libby a bit; she hadn't expected Marc Clayton to be able to speak French like that, and it sounded so damn sexy that she could feel the hairs on the back of her neck starting to prickle with awareness.

'OK, you are in room 411.' Marc turned to look at her and, realising she had been staring at him, she quickly looked away. 'It's on the fourth floor. Do you want me to come up with you?'

'No, I certainly do not,' she said quickly, and snatched up the key card the receptionist had put down for her.

Marc smirked and she had the feeling that really he'd

had no intention of escorting her to her room, but was enjoying winding her up.

'Right, well, I'll see you tonight, then,' he said easily as he glanced at his watch. 'I'll pick you up at seven.'

'I beg your pardon?' She looked up at him blankly.

'I'm taking you for dinner,' he said calmly. 'Had you forgotten?'

'Well…yes, let me see.' She put one finger to her forehead, her tone sardonic. 'I think that might just have slipped my mind in between you hurling insults at me.'

'Hurling insults?' Marc raised an eyebrow. 'Me? I thought we were just getting each other's measure.'

'Well, I got your measure, that's for sure,' Libby said dryly as she reached for her bag that lay beside him on the floor. 'And I certainly don't want to have dinner with you. It would choke me.'

'You are so dramatic.' Mark smiled as if she were the most amusing person he had ever met.

'As well as my being an actor…a gold-digger and, let's see, what other accusations did you hurl?'

'A bit of a temptress?' Mark suggested dryly.

What on earth did he mean by that? Had he recognised the fact that for a few wild seconds in the car she had felt attracted to him? If so, she might as well just curl up now and die of embarrassment. 'What a strange thing to say!' she muttered angrily and hoped vehemently that the colour in her cheeks would be taken for anger, not mortification. 'Why on earth would you think that of me?'

'Maybe it's something to do with the fact that I've noticed you are not afraid to bat those beautiful eyes at me and use your femininity to win a point.' He murmured the words almost seductively and she felt her heart miss several beats as his eyes moved towards her lips. 'It's very…beguiling but, unfortunately for you, I am not fooled by the act for one moment.'

'You know, you talk absolute rubbish.' She managed to say the sentence, but she was half worried that it might come out back to front she was so infuriated. 'And just for the record I have not batted my eyes at you! In fact, I find you so irritating that I'd rather not look at you at all,' she added for good measure.

He smiled. 'So I'll pick you up at seven, then.'

'Are you listening to me? I don't want to have dinner with you—'

'No, I am not listening to you,' he said with lazy humour. 'We have important things to discuss tonight.'

'Like what?' She was momentarily distracted.

'Like your father.' Suddenly Marc's expression was serious. 'There are a few things we need to sort out.'

'What kind of things?'

'We'll discuss that tonight.'

'Look, the only person I want to talk to is my father—'

'And if you care anything about him you will be down here waiting for me at seven.' Marc said the words firmly, then turned away. 'Don't be late.'

Don't be late. Who did he think he was? He sounded like a schoolteacher. Libby turned and headed for the lift. Well, she had told him she didn't want to have dinner with him and she damn well wouldn't. She put her bag down in the lift and pushed the button for the fourth floor.

Before the doors closed she had a last glimpse of Marc Clayton getting into his car outside. And despite the fact that she was so annoyed with him she couldn't help but think how attractive he looked in the casual black T-shirt and the sand-coloured trousers to his suit. She wondered if there was any French blood in him. There was something very Mediterranean about the way he was so stylishly dressed and the darkness of his hair and eyes. And when he had spoken French to the receptionist it had sounded as if it came very naturally to him.

The doors swished closed. She supposed some women would fall for those powerful Mediterranean good looks, but not her. She had Marc Clayton's measure. He was a hateful man, she reminded herself forcefully, leaning back against the wall. *Hateful!* There was no way in a million years that she would fall for someone as arrogant and insufferable as him, that was for sure!

CHAPTER THREE

On the fourth floor Libby picked up her bag and headed out into the corridor. There was no window and it was in total darkness. It took her a moment to find a light switch, and then before she could reach her room the light clicked off leaving her struggling to find her way.

It was a relief when she found her door and stepped inside to find a pretty sun-drenched bedroom in pale primrose. The large windows overlooked a row of bourgeois houses all with balconies covered with tubs of red and pink geraniums.

Libby flung her bag down and went across to look out at the view. It was extraordinary being in France waiting for a reunion with her father, and in some ways it didn't feel quite real. It was as if she had entered some limbo land between her old life and the future. Also it was strange that the reunion should be here in the Côte D'Azur, because this was where they had spent their last family holiday together. Libby only had hazy memories of it, but she remembered they had rented an apartment in Menton and her father had taught her to swim. She remembered how much fun it had been and how patient and loving he had been.

It was when they returned home from that holiday that her parents had separated. There had been no clue to it beforehand, no arguments, no angry atmosphere. One day they had been a happy family…or so she had thought… and the next her father was gone. And a few months later Sean had moved in with her mother. At first Sean had seemed nice, but Libby had quickly learnt that beneath the smiling façade lay a much more sinister character. She had missed her father, had asked for him and that had resulted in a swift and furious response from her mother's new partner. Libby had tried not to ask too many questions after that.

It was a year after her marriage to Sean that her mother had taken her to one side and told her that her father was dead. Libby had had no reason to disbelieve her words. But now she knew her mother had lied. And it was such a cruel thing to do. Why had her usually gentle and loving mother done such a thing? Was it simply to stop her asking for her father? Maybe she had known her father didn't want to see her and it had been some bizarre act of kindness?

These were the questions that were driving her mad and pushing her to make contact with her father. It certainly had nothing to do with money as Marc Clayton had so callously suggested.

Also, now that her mother was dead, her father was her only living relative. Libby's eyes blurred with sudden tears as she thought about this. She still missed her mum; her death had been such a shock. But there was no point thinking about the past, she had to look to the future now.

She wondered when her father would arrive and felt a flutter of apprehension deep inside.

Had he really told Marc Clayton that he had tried to contact her and that she had wanted nothing to do with him, had slammed the door in his face? Why would he tell such a lie? Why would Marc make it up? None of it made sense.

She sighed and leaned her forehead against the window. Maybe she should have dinner with the enemy tonight. It beat sitting alone in a restaurant and maybe she would learn something.

The sudden change of mind swept over her from nowhere; along with the realisation that whether she liked it or not Marc Clayton was her only link to her father. So for the time being she would have to put up with him, but how was she going to do that? The man drove her mad; she needed a strategy, a plan.

She remembered how he'd accused her of using her femininity to gain control of the situation... Well, maybe that wasn't a bad idea! Maybe she could play that game, grit her teeth as he flung insults at her and use some subtle flattery, some eyelash fluttering. He'd said he wasn't fooled by her...well, she would test that theory out.

She smiled to herself as she headed over to unpack. The idea seemed sensible and, OK, she might be playing with fire, but she could handle Marc Clayton, she told herself confidently...couldn't she?

Libby's confidence started to falter as the time approached for her to go downstairs and face Marc again. She gave herself an extra spray of perfume and checked her appearance in the cheval mirror. What to wear shouldn't have been too much of a problem, as she hadn't brought a lot of clothes with her. She had two dresses: one was black and plain, the other butterfly-blue with shoestring shoulder straps. But unfortunately she hadn't been able to make her mind up between them and had tried them both on twice before finally deciding on the blue one.

Not that she cared what Marc Clayton thought of her, of course, but she needed the extra confidence of knowing she looked good. Her eyes flicked critically over her figure. She was constantly battling to keep her weight down. Libby only had to look at a cream cake and it seemed to appear on her hips. And at the moment she did feel as if she were carrying an extra few pounds. The dress, however, seemed to hide that fact. It was summery and feminine and it fitted to the curves of her body in a way that was subtly sexy... It would do, she told herself firmly as she snatched up her purse and left the room.

She arrived downstairs at a few minutes before seven. There was no sign of Marc so she sat on one of the sofas in the reception area and flicked through a magazine, pretending to be cool and calm and collected when in fact she was anything but.

Pull yourself together, Lib, she told herself sharply. He's just a man. You'll have him eating out of your hand by the end of the evening. You can deal with him easily.

'Hi. It's Libby Sheridan, isn't it?' a friendly voice enquired.

Libby glanced up in surprise at a man who was vaguely familiar. She wasn't expecting to see anyone she knew here and she couldn't place him at all. He was wearing jeans and a grey T-shirt. Not bad-looking, blond hair and grey inquisitive eyes. 'Hi.' She half smiled as he walked across the reception towards her. 'Sorry—do I know you?'

'Yes, John Wright. We met last week in a London bar.' He sat down next to her on the sofa and turned to offer his hand.

Libby felt a jolt of shock. 'You're that reporter, aren't you?'

'That's right.' His smile stretched even wider, but he dropped his hand when she didn't take hold of it. 'I gave you my card, remember?'

'Yes, I do. And I told you I couldn't help you,' she said quickly. 'What are you doing here?'

'I'm here with a few friends covering the film festival.'

'And you are staying here, at this hotel?' Libby frowned.

'That's right.' He nodded. 'So tell me—have you made contact with your father yet?'

Libby stared at him in astonishment. 'Have you followed me here?'

'No, of course not. I told you, I'm here for the Cannes Film Festival.'

Libby should have believed him; after all, it was too weird to think a reporter would go to the trouble of following *her* around. But bumping into him twice did seem too much of a coincidence. 'Look, I told you before. I am not interested in talking to you.'

'Oh, come on, Libby, give me a break,' he implored. 'Carl Quinton is hot property at the moment and a story about his reunion with his long-lost daughter would be of tremendous human interest. The tabloids will pay big money. It will definitely be worth your while.'

'You are wasting your time with this.' Libby put her magazine down as she saw Marc walking into the lobby and she got to her feet quickly. She didn't want Marc to see her talking with a reporter. Heaven alone knew what kind of spin he would put on that, but she was willing to bet it would not be good. She remembered his words in the car. 'Maybe you think you can sell your story to the press.'

'Look, if you change your mind.' John Wright also stood up and tried to hand her his card again.

Rather than make a scene she took it. 'Goodbye, Mr Wright,' she said succinctly, turning her attention firmly towards Marc.

He was wearing a dark suit that seemed to emphasise the width of his shoulders and the power of his physique and he looked so handsome that Libby felt her mind going into a weird kind of free fall for a second.

She was acutely conscious of the way he watched her as she walked across to him. No man had ever looked at her with that kind of intensity before; it was as if he was taking in every little detail about her.

'Hi.' He smiled at her, and it was a smile that for a moment lit the darkness of his eyes. 'You look lovely.'

'Thank you.' She was surprised when he leaned closer and kissed her on both cheeks. The touch of his lips against her skin and the scent of his cologne enveloped her in a heady wave of intoxication, sending sensations of pure excitement slithering down her spine. It took all of her strength to step back and smile coolly up at him.

'So who is the guy?' Marc continued swiftly, looking past her to where John Wright was now leaning nonchalantly against the reception desk.

Libby hesitated for half a second. She hated lying, but her inner voice was telling her it was the thing to do. 'Oh, just some English guy who's staying here.' She said the words flippantly. 'We were just passing the time of day.'

'Really.' Marc's voice was dry. 'And which paper does he work for?'

Libby felt her skin heat up as he waited laconically for her answer. 'I have no idea what you are talking about,' she blustered. 'Now, shall we go or are you going to shine a light in my eyes and do a thorough interrogation?'

Marc hesitated and she thought for one awful moment that he was going to go across to talk to the other man. But to her relief he just turned to lead the way out of the hotel.

The warmth of the evening hit her as they stepped outside and it was very welcome after the air-conditioned interior. She noticed that Marc still had the top down on his car and she wished she had remembered to bring a tie for her hair to stop the breeze ruffling it. She hoped it wasn't going to be a complete frizz by the time they reached the restaurant. Marc opened the passenger door for her before going around to the driver's side.

'So how many meetings have you set up while you are here?' he asked casually as he pulled the vehicle out into traffic.

'Meetings?' She forgot about her hair and glanced across at him with a frown.

'Yes, meetings.' He looked at her pointedly. 'With journalists.' He enunciated the words as if speaking to a wayward child. And as he spoke he reached across and pulled the card the reporter had given her from her fingers.

Libby watched as he read it, then threw it away into the blackness of the night, and her skin burned with annoyance. Damn, why hadn't she refused that card?

'If you are auctioning your story to members of the press, then I hope you have bigger fish than him on your hook,' Marc continued smoothly. 'He's not going to pay much.'

'I'm not doing anything of the sort,' Libby muttered angrily.

'So if you are so innocent why did you lie about him being a reporter?'

'Because...' Libby glared at him. 'Well...because, let's face it, if I'd told you I was as surprised to see him there as you were, I didn't think you would have believed me, would you?'

Marc was silent for a moment. 'Probably not,' he conceded.

'Well, there you are. I rest my case.' She shrugged slender shoulders. 'Although, when I think about it, I really don't know why you would be bothered about my speaking to the press anyway.'

He glanced over at her. 'Are you being deliberately naïve?'

'I am not being naïve; I just find the whole thing bizarre. For one thing, I don't know anything about my father's life these days. I haven't seen him since I was seven. I didn't even know where he was until last week…actually, on second thoughts I still don't know where he is now…and I have reporters tracking me down for my story.' She shook her head. 'It's all very strange.'

'You do realise if you give the press a sob story about your father abandoning you, that it could seriously affect his career. His new film, where he plays the part of *a warm and sympathetic family man*, could be a complete flop at the box office.'

Libby looked across at him sharply. 'I would never do anything that would hurt my dad.'

'Well, that's good to know.'

Libby thought she redetected a sardonic note in his voice. 'You are determined to think badly of me, aren't you?' Her eyes blazed brightly as she looked across at him.

He glanced around and for a moment their eyes met. 'No…on the contrary, Libby, I don't want to think badly of you at all.'

The gentleness of his voice caught her off guard, made her feel confused. Hurriedly she looked away from him again.

'You could have fooled me.' She tried to keep her voice crisp, but it had lost its intensity now.

They were driving along the Corniche d'Or, a twisty road that hugged the coast giving spectacular views out across the Mediterranean. A full moon cast a silvery reflection over the road and the sea; the sky was studded with the glitter of a million stars.

'Where are we going?' Libby asked curiously.

'A little country restaurant I know, it's not far away now.'

'Trying to hide me away from the prying eyes of the paparazzi?' She asked the question wryly, still unable to believe that anyone would be interested in her.

'I thought it best to go somewhere quiet where we can talk in peace.'

They turned a corner and a sparkle of light lit the night as they approached a small hamlet perched by the sea. Then Marc turned the car into a car park next to what looked like an intimate little restaurant.

It was probably the kind of place where lovers dined, Libby thought as they stepped through the front door. It had all the ambience of a romantic hideaway. All the tables were set within private wooden booths and the only light was from the candles that flickered there and the soft glow of lanterns that hung in the windows. Once upon a time it might have been a sea captain's house; now its uneven wooden floors had been given a polished sophistication and fresh flowers adorned every table.

They were shown immediately to a booth and Marc ordered some wine. Libby glanced down at the menu she had been handed and noticed there were no prices on anything. Obviously this was the kind of place where it was taken for granted that the man would be paying.

'So what do you fancy to eat?' Marc enquired as he leaned across and filled her glass.

'I'm not sure.' She glanced over at him.

'You did get an English menu, didn't you?'

'Yes, but there are no prices on it.'

'Well, surely you don't need a price to decide what you want to eat, do you?' His voice was grim.

'No, but I just wanted to make it clear that I will be paying for my own meal. I am an independent kind of person and I prefer it that way.'

She could see from the dark glitter in his eyes that this thoroughly amused him. 'Whatever you say, Libby.'

Was he being facetious? Libby stared at him for a moment, unable to make up her mind. He held her gaze steadily, then smiled at her and raised his glass. 'Here's to independent women.' There was a slightly husky, sensual quality to his tone that made tingles of awareness suddenly shoot through her. Hurriedly she looked away from him and back at the menu.

She hated the way he was able to make her feel so...on edge. He was the most infuriating person she had ever met!

The waitress arrived to take their order and Libby transferred her attention towards food. She was surprised to find that she was very hungry, and then she remembered that she hadn't eaten anything today apart from a small bowl of cereal before leaving for the airport this morning.

Marc spoke in fluent French to the waitress; she seemed to know him well and they laughed together about something.

'You speak very good French,' Libby remarked once they were alone again.

'I was brought up here. My mother was from Nice.'

'That explains your Mediterranean looks,' Libby said with a nod. 'Was your father French as well?'

'No, he's English. But after my mother died he stayed on in France; he's very at home here. And I suppose I tend to think of France as my home as well. I have offices here in the Côte d'Azur and a house just outside Nice.'

'Where do you spend the rest of your time?' Libby asked.

'You seem very interested in my private life,' Marc countered the question with a raised eyebrow.

'I was trying to make polite conversation… But on second thoughts…' she shrugged '…I know the answer to that anyway. I've read about you in the papers.'

'Have you now.'

'Yes…just in passing…ages ago,' she added hastily in case he thought she was particularly interested in him.

'So what have you read about me?' he asked lazily.

'Interested in your own publicity?' she responded wryly.

'Interested to see how much research you've done before coming out here.'

'I didn't research you. I read about you casually as lots of other people have.' It was an effort to keep the sharp tone out of her voice. She was supposed to be using her femininity, she reminded herself. 'So let's see—what can I remember…?' She pretended to think. 'Well, I didn't know your mother was French. But I do know you have a beach house in Malibu, California, I believe.' Libby had seen a picture of it as well and, from what she remembered, the place was a huge mansion fronting onto the sea, with massive verandas, a sunken pool and a Jacuzzi, but she didn't bother to tell him she knew that. For some reason she had the distinct impression he might think she had paid attention to those photos for all the wrong reasons. 'And let's see…' Libby paused. 'You are thirty-three and divorced from the film star Marietta. And you have a daughter…I think she would be about two years of age now.'

'Three,' he corrected her.

'Oh, well, it's a while since I read about you.' Libby shrugged. 'Where is your little girl now?'

'My ex-wife and I have joint custody. So Alice spends her time between Marietta's house in Beverly Hills and mine in Malibu.'

'It sounds a pretty civilised arrangement.'

'Yes, it is. Unfortunately we couldn't make our marriage work, but we both adore Alice. She is a very beautiful little girl, clever and sweet-natured. A real ray of sunshine to have around.'

Libby noticed how his manner relaxed and his voice softened as he talked about his daughter. 'Do you have a photo of her?' she asked impulsively.

Marc hesitated for a moment, and then reached into his inside pocket and took out his wallet. He slid across a photo of a little girl with long blonde curly hair and a bright cheeky smile. 'She does look adorable,' Libby said sincerely, then couldn't help adding, 'Obviously she takes after her mother.'

Marc smiled at that. 'Yes, I suppose she does.'

Libby searched her memory and tried to remember what had happened between him and his ex-wife. She remembered their wedding pictures very clearly, remembered thinking what a perfect couple they made. Marc was so very handsome and Marietta...well, she was probably one of the world's most beautiful women, she had a figure to die for and long wheat-blonde hair. But although Libby could remember those pictures she couldn't remember anything about the divorce except something about Marc paying a huge settlement.

She slid the photo back to him. 'You must miss her while you are here in France.'

'Yes, but she is arriving soon with Marietta, so she will be coming up to spend a few nights at my house.'

'Who—Marietta or Alice?' Libby asked, wondering just how civilised their arrangement was.

'Alice. Marietta will be very busy. She is staying in Cannes for the film festival.'

'I would have thought it would be a very busy time for you as well.'

'It is, but I have a lot of back-up here. My father and my sisters all want to have Alice over to stay with them.'

'So you have a whole host of ready and willing baby-sitters.'

'Yes. That's right, and they are all really looking forward to seeing her again.' He put the photo away. 'So...what about you?' Marc asked suddenly. 'Have you ever taken the matrimonial plunge?'

Libby shook her head. 'No, I've never been married.' For a moment she found herself thinking about Simon. She had really thought that he was the 'one' and that they would have married and had children and lived happily ever after.

In honesty, if she had known up front that he hadn't wanted children she probably would never have agreed to live with him, because she was a person who wanted a family life. But Simon had lied to her by omission, always managing to dodge the issue. And later, when she had discovered the truth, she had been too far into the relationship to want to extricate herself from it.

So she had made excuses for him, told herself that because he'd had a few broken relationships in the past he was just frightened by the thought of such a huge commitment, that if she was warm and patient and helped him to see how wonderful things could be in a loving relationship he would come around to the idea of having children in his own time. And she had really believed that, because she had believed that he had loved her.

'Libby?' Marc's gentle voice brought her quickly back to the present.

'Sorry. I was miles away.'

'What were you thinking about?'

'Nothing much.' Libby was glad that their food arrived at that moment. She certainly didn't want to tell Marc that she had been thinking about what an idiot she had been in the past. She could hardly bear to acknowledge the fact to herself, let alone tell *him*. Libby ran a distracted hand through her hair. She had always thought she was an intelligent woman and yet where love was concerned her brains seemed to scramble. Hell, there had even been months when she had carried Simon financially...not to mention the credit-card debacle. She had cancelled that card before leaving for France, but from what she could gather she seemed to have funded a whole new kitchen and helped him set up in his new home wherever that was! And he hadn't returned any of her calls to talk about it.

'And is there a special man waiting for you back in London?' Marc leaned across and poured her a glass of wine.

Libby hesitated. She was by nature a truthful person, but for some reason, maybe pride, she didn't want to tell this man that there was no one in her life. She wanted to hide from him behind a warm and happy façade...

'Oh, yes...' Libby shrugged. 'Simon and I have been together for three years now. We are very happy.'

As she glanced over and met the darkness of Marc's eyes she wished she hadn't added that last bit...it was perhaps a bit over the top.

Before Marc could ask anything further she swiftly changed the subject. 'So when will my father be arriving in town?'

'He's in the States at the moment finishing a tour of the chat shows to promote his film. He'll be here directly after that.'

'Gosh! You're getting very brave telling me where he is!' Libby looked across at him teasingly. 'Aren't you afraid I might misuse the information, try to sell it on the Internet or something?'

'Well, maybe I've decided it's time to start living dangerously where you are concerned.' Marc matched her light bantering tone exactly. 'In any case, most people will be catching him on cable tomorrow night anyway.'

'Shucks—no profit to be made in spilling that secret, then.'

'Afraid not.'

Libby tasted her salad; it was absolutely delicious. 'This is lovely.'

'Yes, the food is always good in here.'

Libby wondered whom he usually brought to dine with him here. He was so good-looking there had to be a woman in his life, maybe even a whole string of them. As she looked across at him she wondered what it would be like to be dated by Marc Clayton. Not that she was his type, of course; he probably only went for stick thin model girls. She frowned, annoyed by the thought. She didn't care what Marc Clayton thought of her, she reminded herself firmly, because she didn't even like the man. But she did need him to reach her father, she reminded herself sharply, and that meant swallowing her pride and being nice to him.

'So you've decided to live dangerously where I'm concerned.' She smiled at him and lowered her tone to a slightly husky note. 'That sounds promising. Does that mean you are going to tell me where my father will be staying when he arrives?'

'I don't see why not.' Marc's voice was equally low, equally warm and husky.

Maybe she could get to like him after all, she thought hazily as she looked into his eyes. 'Good. I'm glad we can be civil about this.'

'Absolutely.' Marc smiled. 'All you need to do is go along with my plans and prove to me that you do have your father's best interests at heart, and I will help your reunion in every way I can.'

The lazily arrogant words set fire to Libby's good feelings. Her eyes narrowed on him. 'I don't have to prove anything to you.' The words were out before she could stop them.

'Well, I think you do. You see, your father hired me to look after his best interests and that is what I intend to do.'

The waitress arrived to clear the table and bring their main course. There was a stony silence as she served them. Libby was desperately trying to rein in her temper.

As they were left alone again Marc leaned across and topped up her wineglass.

'Don't look at me with those distressed blue eyes, Libby, because I'm not going to fall for your injured-party look. I have a duty of care towards your father—'

'Don't give me that holier-than-thou routine, Marc Clayton, because it isn't washing,' Libby muttered. 'I am not stupid. I know damn well that you have probably invested a lot of money promoting my father's career and his new film and the only duty of care you are worried about is to your profit margins.'

Marc shrugged, not one bit put out by her remark. 'Yes, I'm a businessman...and, yes, I have spent a lot of money promoting your father's career. But I also happen to like your father and I think of him as a friend. So, any way round you like to look at it, I'm not going to let you ruin things for him.'

'And I've told you I am not going to ruin anything for him.'

'Well, good, then we are both in agreement and there is no problem.'

The very smoothness of his tone irritated Libby. 'So now we are in agreement, are you going to put me in direct contact with my father? I want to talk to him,' she said succinctly.

Marc inclined his head. 'As soon as he arrives I will arrange a meeting.'

'You like being in control, don't you?'

'That's the way it is, Libby,' Marc answered her calmly.

'How is he, anyway?' she asked suddenly, looking over at Marc, her eyes wide with curiosity.

'He's fine, very excited about seeing you again.'

So why couldn't he have rung her himself to tell her that? Libby wondered.

'And in the meantime I think we should go over exactly what you are going to tell the press.'

Libby put her knife and fork down and pushed the plate away. 'I'm not going to tell them anything.'

'Yes, well, that might be a mistake. I think we should face the problem head-on rather than back away from it.'

'There is no problem...except in your very fertile imagination,' Libby muttered.

'OK, so remind me again, was that a journalist at your hotel or was it just a figment of my imagination?'

Libby scowled at him.

'You remind me of a schoolgirl. I think it must be those freckles over your nose. All you need to do right now is put that hair of yours in bunches and you'd be perfect.'

'Very funny.' Libby put a self-conscious hand up to her hair and wondered suddenly if it was sitting OK. She had meant to go to the cloakroom and check her appearance as soon as they had arrived and she had forgotten.

'You're very like your father,' Marc remarked suddenly. 'He always likes to be right as well. You've got the same fiery temperament, same dramatic colouring, except of course you are much...much more beautiful.'

The husky way he said those last few words caused Libby's heart rate to increase. It wasn't that she was taken in by the compliment. Marc was just a smooth operator; he'd say that kind of thing to any woman... No, it was more the way he was looking at her that really caused havoc with her emotions. There was something about the way his dark eyes held hers and then slowly, almost provocatively moved to rest on her lips that made her blood pressure soar. Desperately she tried to fight down the raw attraction that seemed to spring up inside her from nowhere and concentrate instead on the more annoying aspects of his words. 'You mean you try and boss my father around as well?'

Marc laughed at that. 'Well, every now and then I try...but like you he is incredibly stubborn.'

The waitress came to clear the table and Libby used the time to escape from Marc to try and clear her head. She checked her appearance in the bright lights of the restroom. Thankfully her hair hadn't turned to frizz and was sitting relatively smoothly. Not that she really cared what she looked like, of course... Marc Clayton wasn't her type; he was far too assertive and insulting. She re-applied her lipstick and remembered how he had made her feel when his gaze had rested on her lips... To her horror her hand trembled a little. She flicked the lipstick closed and put it away.

You *are* attracted to him! The words lashed through her brain like a very loud accusation. And she couldn't deny them at all. OK, she found him attractive...of course she did. He was a very handsome man and, more than that, there was a raw sensuality about him that seemed to stir her in a way no other man had ever done. Something happened when he looked at her in a certain way. She disliked him intensely and yet he excited her, set her adrenalin racing and her pulse sky-high. It was very strange and more than a little worrying. An attraction had to be based on more than good looks, more than the ability to turn your insides to molten fire. How could she feel like this about someone she really didn't like?

You are being ridiculous, Libby, she told herself firmly. You can't be attracted to him...not even sexually! For a start the man thinks you are a gold-digger! He has said horrible things to you and he is trouble with a capital T.

OK, every now and then there was a charisma about him that fascinated her. But she had learnt from her mistakes in the past and she would never, *ever* allow herself to be taken in by any man again. From now on she was a new woman, strong, ruled by her head, not her heart. And she had Marc Clayton's measure, that was for sure.

Another thing for sure was that trying to use her femininity on him was backfiring major style. As soon as she lowered her voice huskily or tried to flirt with him he responded in a similar style and it seemed that his smooth masculinity was more overpowering than her weak flirtations.

She was going to have to play things very carefully.

CHAPTER FOUR

LIBBY took a deep breath and steeled herself to return to the table.

As she was leaving the room a very attractive blonde of a similar age to herself bumped straight into her.

'Pardon, *madame!*' The woman stepped back apologetically.

'It's OK, I'm fine.' Libby smiled at her.

'Ah, you are English, are you not?'

Why was it that when a Frenchwoman spoke in broken English it was the most attractive sound? Libby was certain the same couldn't be said for her when she spoke in her stumbling French.

'Yes, I am.' She nodded.

'I noticed you in the dining room.'

It was strange, but Libby hadn't noticed her...but then she had been concentrating so hard on what Marc had been saying to her that she hadn't really noticed anybody.

'Tell me, is that Marc Clayton you are dining with?'

'Eh...yes,' Libby answered in surprise.

'I thought so...he is very attractive.'

'I suppose so—' Before Libby could finish the woman had swept on by and into the bathroom.

With a frown Libby returned to her table. She supposed that a lot of people would recognise Marc, he was a high-profile celebrity in his own right.

She was going to tell Marc about the incident, but as soon as she resumed her seat opposite him he continued briskly, 'Anyway, getting back to the subject in hand.'

'Yes? What was that?' Libby asked distractedly.

'I think you should give the press a short statement, something along the lines of how much you love your father and how circumstances have kept you apart. You don't need to go into details—'

'Oh, I see.' He had her full attention now. 'Perhaps you'd like to write a speech for me, put a bit of emotional spin in there while you are at it,' she suggested dryly.

'Emotional spin...' Marc pretended to think about that for a moment, and then smiled at her. 'Now, what do you suggest?'

'Oh, I don't know.' Libby waved her hand airily. 'I'll leave that up to you, shall I? Because, judging by the things you have been saying to me, you do seem to have a remarkably vivid imagination. Maybe you could tell everyone I was lost at sea and spent twenty years living on a desert island? '

'Yes, well, from your point of view I suppose that beats telling the truth,' Marc said, cutting across her sarcasm dismissively. 'That you have wanted nothing to do with your father until now and the only thing driving your little reunion is the fact that he now happens to be in the media spotlight and the money.'

Libby felt her skin heat with fury at those insulting words. There, she told herself furiously. Now he was showing his true colours again! 'That is your version of the truth,' she told him tightly, 'and it is way off line.'

'Bit more believable than your desert-island excuse, though,' Marc replied nonchalantly.

Libby's temperature felt as if it had shot through the ceiling now. 'I don't have to make excuses for my behaviour, because I haven't done anything wrong.' Her eyes blazed into his.

'If you say so.' Marc's tone was infuriatingly calm.

Libby wanted to storm out of there and have nothing more to do with him. It seemed the safest option as well! Hastily she pulled herself together, but it took every ounce of her self-control to rein in her temper and remind herself that Marc was her only real link with her father and walking out on him right now wasn't really an option.

'So what are you going to tell the press, then?' She forced herself to ask the question calmly.

'Well, certainly not that your credit rating is low,' he replied nonchalantly.

Libby's face was on fire with fury now. 'There's nothing wrong with my credit rating,' she blustered.

'There is according to my research.'

Libby stared at him in consternation. 'What research?'

'Oh, I've got a dossier on you this thick.' Marc held his hand twelve inches off the table. 'I put a private investigator on the case.'

Libby was so shocked she could hardly speak. 'I hope that is a joke?' she spluttered.

'No.' In contrast to her, Marc sounded coolly composed. 'Firstly I needed to make sure you were who you said you were. And secondly I wanted to know as much about you as possible so that I knew who I was dealing with.'

'Really?' Libby's head was reeling with this information. 'So you know all about my misspent youth, then?' She tried to make a joke, but her voice was filled with arid disdain.

'Unfortunately my investigator missed that bit out.' Marc leaned his head in his hands and fixed her with a very interested look. 'Would you like to tell me about it? I promise it will go no further.'

'Much as I'm sure you are the soul of discretion, I think

I'll pass, thanks, just in case it gets incorporated into the little speech you are preparing for the press on my behalf.'

'Pity.' Marc shrugged. 'I think I might have enjoyed that piece of information. I did learn, however, that you and your boyfriend Simon have split up...which begs the question why you lied to me about that earlier?'

The nonchalant question made her stomach churn. She never usually told lies...it was just her luck that when she did she was instantly found out! And by Marc Clayton of all people, he already had a lower-than-low opinion of her. With difficulty she held his gaze. 'I didn't lie. We are just having a break from each other, that's all! And we are making plans now to get back together—not that it is any of your damn business.'

'Ordinarily I would agree. But I got to wondering why you had split up, and when I saw the state of your finances I couldn't help wondering if Simon's departure had anything to do with the fact that you are hopeless with money...a compulsive shopper, I believe.'

'You know, Marc, I think you are quite obsessed with the subject of money.' Her eyes burned into his. 'And I hate to disappoint you, but your theory is wrong. Money had nothing whatsoever to do with Simon and I taking a break! And I am not a compulsive shopper.'

'But you are all spent up,' he reflected. 'So I suppose that was when you decided to come and find Daddy?'

Libby was so furious now that she wanted to reach out and wipe that infuriating, smug, know-it-all expression off his face. She linked her hands together and reined in tight control.

'Your remarks are insulting and absurd!' She glared at him. 'And do you know what? I'm not even going to grace them any further with an answer.'

She was quite proud of the fact that her voice was now

very cool and her manner poised. There was no way she was going to allow this man to upset her further.

Marc met her eyes across the table. He had to admit, her cool dignity was impressive. Hell, the way she looked at him with those big blue eyes even made him feel momentarily guilty! He frowned. Why should he feel guilty? She was the trickster here... He had already caught her out on two lies this evening. 'I'm sorry I had to pry, Libby. But for your father's sake I had to check you out.'

She glanced at her watch. 'If you don't mind, I'd like to go now.'

'Go?'

'Yes, back to my hotel. It's been rather a long day.'

'You haven't eaten much. Why don't you let me order you something else?'

Libby was surprised that he had noticed how much she had eaten, and was even more taken aback by that sudden note of concern in his voice... It was fake, of course.

'I'm fine. I really enjoyed the meal. It was just the company that was a bit dodgy.' She flashed him a pointed look from bright blue eyes and shrugged. 'But you can't have everything, can you?'

'So they say.' Marc seemed not in the least put out by the remark. 'Though I've never held with that sentiment myself.'

No, he wouldn't, Libby thought as she watched him put up a hand to summon the waitress over. Marc Clayton was obviously very used to having it all. There was an unmistakable air of power and determination about him that stated very clearly that he got what he wanted. She still couldn't believe he'd had the audacity to put a private detective on her!

The bill was produced and Marc put his credit card down on the silver tray provided.

'So how much do I owe you?' Libby asked quickly.

Marc waved a hand dismissively. 'Let's just put it on the account, shall we?'

'What account?'

'The account to be settled at a later date.' He looked over at her and smiled. 'By me.'

'I'd rather not, thank you.' She hoped she didn't sound too prim, but there was no way she was going to be under an obligation to him. Quickly she stretched out a hand and took the bill from the plate.

As she glanced down at it she thought for a moment that she was looking at a VAT number or the till-receipt number... The meal surely couldn't have cost that much? But, no, as she scanned the list she saw that the bottom number was indeed the correct total. She certainly didn't have enough cash on her to even pay half!

She glanced over at him and half smiled. 'I'll have to give you my credit card.'

Marc reached out and took the bill back from her. 'I invited you to dinner, Libby, and I am paying.'

'Certainly not!' Hastily she scrabbled for her purse, produced her credit card and dropped it onto the silver plate along with his. 'There.' She smiled at him. 'Just split it between the two cards.' She was pleased by how non-chalant her voice sounded, as if the amount was nothing to her.

For a moment Marc's eyes held with hers across the table. He noticed the defiant sparkle in her gaze and the erect way she held herself so ramrod-straight in her chair. Then he stood up. 'I'm not fooled for one moment by that act, Libby.' He tossed her credit card back on the table. 'Save your "little miss independent" charade for your father.'

Before she could answer him he had walked away to take the bill towards a small reception area.

Libby glared at his retreating, broad back. 'Loathsome man,' she muttered, putting her card away.

A few moments later Marc made his way back to the table. He had a grim expression on his face.

'Everything OK?' She gritted her teeth and forced herself to sound civil.

'Not really,' he muttered. 'The paparazzi are out at the front of the restaurant so we had better leave by the back exit.'

'Really?' Libby was astounded.

'Yes, really. So what I suggest is that I leave the table first and, just in case they can see us through the windows, you give me a few minutes before following.'

Libby shook her head. 'I can't believe they have followed us out here.'

'Well, they are definitely out there. I'll see you outside in five minutes.'

Was this really necessary? There was no time to ask; Marc was already moving away from the table.

She sat for the required amount of time and tried not to glance towards the windows. Then she stood up and followed the direction Marc had taken towards the back of the restaurant. This really was strange. Who would ever have thought that she would be fleeing the paparazzi through a back door? Surely it wasn't because of her? Maybe they were more interested in Marc?

Their waitress was waiting for her by the back door and she opened it for her with a smile. Then Libby found herself in a moonlit garden fragrant with the scent of lavender. Just beyond the dark, neat rows of flowerbeds, the sea was a silver and charcoal mosaic of light.

'Over here.' Marc was waiting for her by a gate.

'This is ridiculous,' Libby muttered as she made her way across to him. 'Are you sure the paparazzi are out at the front? I can't understand why they would be bothered to follow us like this.'

'They didn't follow us. Someone has tipped them off, told them we are here.'

Libby stopped in her tracks. 'I hope you are not suggesting that I did that! Because I'm getting really tired of you throwing these accusations at me!' She put one hand on her hip. 'I did not tip the press off.'

Marc turned and looked down at the bright sparkle of anger in her eyes. 'You know, I was right! You really should take up acting. You can be very convincing.'

'I'm telling you, Marc, I haven't tipped them off.'

'So you haven't got a mobile phone in your handbag? And you didn't rush off from the table to use it a little while ago?'

'No, I did not! Why would I?'

'Because you are playing a very dangerous game.' Marc's voice was harsh and grating and as he stepped closer Libby swallowed down a feeling of trepidation…but she wasn't sure if the feeling was generated by his mood or by how dangerously attractive she found him.

'I don't know what you are talking about.' She tried to take a step away from him, but he caught hold of her arm. The touch of his skin against hers made her temperature start to rise.

'It's called playing two ends to the middle. You are hoping to get money out of the press…and hoping your father coughs up to shut you up. I suppose another word for it is blackmail, Libby.'

Libby brushed his hand away from her furiously. 'How dare you say something so repugnant?'

'How dare you ring the press?'

'I told you I didn't.'

'Well, that's strange, because I sent our waitress outside to see what was going on, and the paparazzi told her they had received a phone call from a woman about twenty minutes ago... About the same time as you left the table.'

'Well, it's a coincidence!' Libby spluttered indignantly.

'Just like the journalist at your hotel was a coincidence as well?'

'Well...yes...I can't explain it...'

'No, I didn't think you could.' Marc reached out and pulled her even closer. Libby felt her heart thud heavily against her chest as she suddenly became aware of the touch of his hand against her waist now.

'You see, the thing is...' Marc reached out and tipped her face gently upwards with one finger under her chin '...that people who play with fire should expect to get burnt.' Although his touch was gentle, his voice was rough like sandpaper on her senses.

Libby couldn't find her voice to be able to make a reply. She could hardly think straight because his fingers were stroking lightly against the side of her face and the butterfly-soft caress was doing very strange things to her emotions. The scent of his cologne mingled with the scent of lavender in the air and it intoxicated her senses.

'What do you want, Marc?' The question was no more than a whisper in the softness of the night air.

'I want you to keep away from the press,' he grated, 'and do as you are damn well told.'

From somewhere she summoned up enough strength of spirit to put defiance in her tone. 'I've never been one for doing what I'm told.'

'Now *that* I believe.' For a second his lips twisted in a ruggedly handsome smile.

'And I won't be bullied or distracted away from what I have come to France to do, and that is see my father.'

'I have no intention of bullying you,' Marc said wryly. 'And I think you are the one who is employing distraction tactics...' For a moment his eyes flicked down over the provocative way her dress showed just a hint of her curves. 'You've deliberately worn a very sexy dress tonight and you know exactly what you are doing every time you moisten your lips...bat your long eyelashes at me.'

'That is absolute rubbish.' Her voice trembled a little and she cursed herself for the sudden loss of composure. But it was really hard to think straight when he was saying things like that...and looking at her with such intensity.

A soft breeze blew a strand of her hair across her face and he reached out a hand to brush it back. The touch of his skin against hers sent tingles of awareness rushing through her.

'Is it?' He shook his head. 'Maybe you just need to learn a little lesson about playing with fire...hmm?'

'Marc, I—'

Whatever else she had been going to say was cut short as his lips crushed down against hers in a ruthlessly punishing kind of kiss.

She should have pushed him away! But the strange thing was that an instant flame of passion flared as soon as their lips met, a flame that was so intense that it spun all the way through Libby's body making her feel weak with a raging desire.

Her hands curled upwards around his neck and she found herself kissing him back with equal hungry intensity.

The moment was slightly unreal. The sound of the sea breaking on the beach below them thundered now in her ears, and all that seemed to matter were the wonderful sensations of desire that he was stirring up inside her. His lips were wildly intoxicating; his hands as they stroked over the side of her face and then moved down her back were masterfully confident and yet so gentle that they melted every inch of her. She longed to be closer to him…longed for so much more…

Then suddenly the dark velvet softness of the night was torn apart by bright flashes of light. Libby stumbled back from Marc in shock and he reached to take hold of her hand as men holding cameras, asking questions, surrounded them.

'No comment, guys,' Marc called as he tried to shelter her from them and hurry her away through the gate out into the car park.

He sounded so together, Libby thought hazily as she got into the car. How was that, when she felt totally dazed…totally out of her depth?

'Who is the young lady, Marc?' One of the reporters shouted the question as Marc backed the car up. 'Are you going to let us in on the secret? Is she Carl Quinton's daughter?'

'She is nobody of any importance to you,' Marc shouted back at them, and then with a squeal of brakes they drove off into the night.

CHAPTER FIVE

NOBODY of any importance! The words drummed through Libby's senses as the car sped through the night.

'They were persistent.' She finally found her voice, but it was shaky in the extreme. She hoped Marc would put that fact down to the circumstance of running from the reporters, and not on the circumstances surrounding their kiss, because anything else would be too embarrassing.

She couldn't believe that she had responded to him like that.

'I don't think they got a clear photo of us,' Marc replied nonchalantly.

'No, and of course telling them that I'm just a nobody will really throw them off the scent.' Her voice was brittle with sarcasm and she could feel anger thundering through her in waves. But she didn't know whom she was more furious with: herself for kissing him like that, or him for saying something so coldly insulting…so coolly flippant after such an intensely passionate moment. But of course that kiss had meant nothing to him; he had merely been toying with her, a bit as a lion might toy with its prey. The knowledge intensified her anger, and also curiously she was aware of a dull kind of raw ache springing up inside her from nowhere.

He glanced across at her. 'I didn't put it quite like that. I said you were nobody as far as *they* were concerned.'

'I think that amounts to the same thing, doesn't it?' she said coolly.

'I was just trying to keep you out of the press.' He

glanced over at her again. 'But you don't want that, do you?' His voice hardened. 'You want to be centre stage in all this.'

'No, I do not!' She curled her fingers into tight fists.

'I'm telling you, Libby, no matter how much interest you try to whip up with the press, you won't make that much money from selling your story. You will be a two-minute wonder.'

'I've got you worried, though, haven't I?' Libby couldn't resist the jibe.

'I'm concerned, not worried,' Marc retorted sharply. 'This is a very important time for your father...but then you are well aware of that, aren't you? You know exactly what you are doing.'

'All I want to do is see him,' she muttered. 'I don't think that is unreasonable.'

'No, it's not. And as long as you play by my rules, I will arrange that for you.'

'Your rules?' Her voice trembled slightly. 'I don't know who the hell you think you are, ordering me around...pouncing on me!'

'Pouncing on you?' There was a hint of amusement in Marc's tone now.

'You had no right to kiss me like that,' she muttered.

'It was just a kiss, Libby.' He said the words gently, and then glanced around at her. 'You could have pulled away...but you didn't. In fact, I would go so far as to say that you enjoyed it.'

'Oh, you think so, do you?' He really was an arrogant so-and-so! Well, she would knock him down a peg or two and enjoy it. 'For your information, actually, I was going to pull away.' She smiled at him as their eyes met. 'But I saw the press approaching and I thought why not give them something to photograph?'

'I see.' Marc looked back at the road. 'It was a convincing act, I'll give you that.'

She was slightly mollified to hear that his tone had lost a little of its cool arrogance. Good! She sincerely hoped that she had dented some of that male ego. There was no way that she wanted him to know just how much he had turned her on. It was far…far too embarrassing.

'So is this your way of admitting that it was you who tipped the paparazzi off?'

His insouciant question made her momentary feeling of triumph disappear very quickly.

'No! It certainly is not!' she said quickly. 'I told you I didn't phone the press.'

'Right.' Marc's voice was filled with dry disbelief. 'You just played up for the paparazzi out of a philanthropic need to give them something more juicy to photograph.'

'Listen, if we are going to get pedantic, you kissed me first!' she retorted swiftly. 'Maybe you phoned the press and were milking it for every penny.'

'And why would I do that?'

'I don't know.' Libby sought about wildly in her brain. 'Maybe you thought you'd give the situation some emotional spin. Distract the press from the real story by throwing in a bit of a good old-fashioned love interest?'

'Very amusing!' Marc shook his head. 'I can assure you, Libby, that I have no intention of giving you a public seal of approval. For one thing I have my position as your father's agent and publicist to consider.'

'Wouldn't want to demean yourself in the press's eyes with a mere nobody, you mean? Sorry…silly me.' Libby's voice grated dryly. 'You really are quite a pompous stuffed shirt, aren't you?' She glared out towards the sea, and was furious with herself for feeling upset. What on earth was wrong with her? She knew perfectly well that Marc had a low opinion of her and, OK, so she had enjoyed being kissed by him! That had been a mistake…a stupid…stupid mistake! But it was just a kiss and better forgotten!

'I'm a businessman first and foremost, Libby,' he retorted bluntly. 'And I suggest you bear that in mind before you play any more games. If there are to be winners and losers in this, then I have no intention of being the loser.'

Libby made no reply, just continued to stare out to sea. She was willing to bet that Marc Clayton never lost, that he was prepared to be as ruthless as it took to get exactly what he wanted.

'I think under the circumstances that we should move you out of your hotel straight away.'

The sudden suggestion made her look back at him in surprise. 'Certainly not! I can't see the point in that at all,' Libby said quickly.

'The point is that the press are all over you already. It is only going to get worse.'

'Well, that is a chance I'm willing to take.'

'I'm sure you are,' Marc said laconically. 'But it's not one I want to take. No, I want you where I can keep an eye on you.'

'That's as may be, but I'm not moving out of my hotel.'

'If you want to see your father, you will do as you are told.'

'Now who is using blackmail?' Libby gave a shaky, incredulous laugh.

'This is for your benefit as well as your father's.'

'And I really believe that!' Libby muttered sardonically.

'I have a house not far from my own; I keep it for special clients who need privacy when they are over here on business. The security is very tight there. It has electric fences and gates, and it is run by a very trustworthy staff.'

'You want to lock me away behind electric fences?' Libby was enraged. 'You must be joking! That's a bit like being sent to prison, isn't it? Well, you can forget that!'

'No, I won't forget it and I'm deadly serious.'

'Well, so am I when I say that I wouldn't want to move into your house if it was the last place with a roof left on the Côte D'Azur.'

'I can assure you that the arrangement will be perfectly civilised and it will be nothing like being in prison.' Marc sounded lazily amused by her vehemence, before continuing firmly, 'The house is the last word in luxury with magnificent views over the Mediterranean and a heated outdoor swimming pool. You can come and go as you please and you will have your own cook, cleaners and chauffeur.'

She was momentarily distracted. It sounded too good to be true. 'And it would all just be for me...?'

'Yes.'

'There would be nobody else in the entire house except for me and the staff?' She checked again.

'That's correct.' Marc smiled to himself. He wanted her out of Cannes and away from the press and he felt he had her within sights of his hook now. He glanced around at her and added casually, 'I'll be there now and again, of course. The house is next door to mine and has a connecting private beach.'

Alarm bells rang very loudly inside Libby. She couldn't help remembering the way Marc had kissed her and the wild passion that had taken them over. It was imperative that she kept her distance from him! 'So what will you be doing; dropping over to collect the rent?' she asked dryly.

'I might have known that the first thing you'd think about would be money. You will of course be able to stay there free of charge.'

Libby opened her mouth to say that she hadn't actually been thinking about money, and then closed it again. It was too embarrassing to broach what had momentarily flicked through her mind.

There was a moment's silence.

'The arrangement will be completely above board,' Marc said suddenly. 'If that's what's bothering you.'

'I didn't for one moment think anything else!' she lied.

'Didn't you?' he flicked a wryly amused glance in her direction and she tried without success not to blush.

'I would just rather stay where I am,' she said firmly and looked away from him hurriedly.

'Why?'

The blunt question annoyed her. 'Because that is where I want to be.'

'Because it's where you told the press you'd be?'

'No!' She shrugged. 'I just think that it is best that you and I keep our distance.'

'You'll be in a separate house to me,' Marc said dryly. 'How much distance do you want?'

As they left the darkness of the coast road behind and entered the bright lights of the city Marc slowed the car and changed down a gear. His hand brushed against her arm as he moved. It was just a casual, accidental touch of his skin again hers, but it immediately sent a hot sense of awareness racing through Libby's whole body.

Separate planets would probably be too close, for her peace of mind, she thought with a sense of annoyance. She hated the fact that he had this power over her senses. How could she let such a hateful man set her pulses racing like this?

'There is absolutely no reason why you should want to stay on in that hotel of yours, except for the fact that you are playing games with me and with the press,' Marc continued with annoyance.

'I am doing no such thing. And…anyway there is another reason why I want to stay in my hotel. It's convenient.'

'Not as convenient as having your own chauffeur.'

'Even so…' She sought around for something else to throw in. 'I do have my reputation to think about.' It was the first thing that came into her mind. 'For all we know pictures of us kissing could be splashed all over the papers tomorrow and then if I move into the house next door to you…well…people will start to put two and two together and reach five, won't they?'

'I don't think so. Why should they?'

'Well…because of the papers—'

'The papers are more interested in your relationship with your father, Libby. Nobody will think there is anything going on between us.'

Libby bit down on the softness of her lip, and something…maybe some spark of pride…made her add, 'Yes, well, my boyfriend might not take such a relaxed view of things, and if he finds out about that kiss and then hears I've moved from my hotel, he might not be so easily persuaded that nothing is going on between us.' She smiled to herself, pleased by the quick-thinking reply. OK, she wasn't an important celebrity, but she wasn't going to let Marc Clayton think that no one gave a damn about her.

'Well, maybe you should have thought about that before you kissed me,' Marc said dismissively.

'Well, maybe I should,' she grated. 'But I have no intention of making things worse by moving out of my hotel and into a house that you own. That could be seen in a much more serious light,' she blustered. 'That could really rock things badly between Simon and I. And I don't need any further complications in my life.'

Marc shrugged, 'I really don't think the press will play up a romantic connection between us; if you were moving into *my* house, not the house next door maybe they would be interested. However, if they do print something and your ex really loves you, maybe it will just make him all the keener. Might even make him regret letting you go in the first place.' Marc slanted a wry look across at her. 'But then perhaps you already thought of that when you rang the press?' he added wryly. 'Maybe you thought you'd kill two birds with one stone?'

'Do you think I spend all my time dreaming up ways of manipulating people?' Libby grated, wildly irritated by the remark.

'I think you are a woman of hidden depths.'

'Just because you are deep and devious doesn't mean everyone else is,' she muttered.

Marc smiled at that. 'Well, if I thought the woman I loved was seeing someone else I'd be doing something about it…and pretty quickly. Even if that something was just calling to ask what was going on.'

'Yes, well, I won't hold my breath on that.' Libby hadn't meant to say those words aloud. So much for keeping her pride, she thought angrily.

'Then he's not worthy of you and you should forget him,' Marc said gently.

Libby frowned. He was just playing games, of course…pretending to be sympathetic for a moment. She wasn't going to be taken in by that.

'Even though I'm a cold-blooded gold-digger?' She muttered the words unevenly.

Marc glanced over at her and smiled. 'Yes…well, you are also a very attractive woman,' he murmured with wry humour.

Libby wished that his husky, teasing tone had no effect on her, but unfortunately just the lazy inflection in his tone had a swirling, confusing effect on her emotions. But she managed to push the feeling to one side and regain some composure. 'Coming from someone who is probably a compulsive womanizer, I won't let your compliments go to my head,' she retorted sarcastically.

Marc laughed at that.

Hell, he even had the most attractive laugh! Life just wasn't fair, Libby thought hazily as she strove for immunity. She felt tired now and emotionally drained. And suddenly she was longing for the peace and tranquillity of her hotel room.

'So shall I pick you up at about ten tomorrow morning?' Marc asked calmly.

'What for?' Libby frowned.

'I told you. To move you into my safe house,' he replied calmly.

'I don't need a safe house!' She shook her head.

'And I think you do.'

'Well, I don't think that my moving out of the hotel will help anything. In fact, it will just complicate things further.'

'I'll worry about the complications. You just pack your stuff and be ready for me to pick you up tomorrow morning at ten.' Marc's tone was uncompromising. He pulled the car up outside her hotel. 'And don't talk to the press until I get here.'

'I wish you would stop telling me what to do.' She glared at him. 'Because I really—'

Anything else she had been about to say was cut off as he leaned across towards her.

'Marc—' Her words were silenced by the softness of his lips. She tried to make herself pull back from him, tried not to return his kisses, but they were so tenderly provocative that she could feel herself starting to surrender, starting to melt towards him. Just at the moment when she knew she was lost and started to kiss him back, he pulled away.

'What was that for?' She looked up at him breathlessly.

'I suppose I wanted to check and see just how much of that last kiss really was for the press's benefit,' he said softly.

'Dented your ego, did I?' She managed to make a flippant reply, but she couldn't tear her eyes away from his; they seemed to hold her spellbound. She could hear her heart thundering against her chest and she hoped sincerely that he couldn't hear it too because it was wildly out of control…a little like her emotions.

He smiled at her. 'No…not in the slightest, because I don't think the press had anything to do with the way you kissed me before. I think chemistry is a much more realistic explanation.'

Libby shook her head, and desperately tried to clear her senses. 'You really are an arrogant so-and-so, Marc Clayton. And I hate to be the bearer of bad news, but the truth is your kiss left me cold. Other women may fall at your feet, but frankly I'm not like other women.'

'Yes, I think I already gathered that much.' He sounded very amused. 'But if that is your response when left cold…I can't wait to warm you up.'

Libby reached angrily for the door handle. 'Just…just keep away from me, Marc.' There was a definite wobble in her voice and she cursed herself for it.

His smile grew. 'I'll see you in the morning. Pleasant dreams.'

'After the night I've had I'll probably be beset by nightmares.' She tossed the words at him over her shoulder and walked away.

Marc watched her go, admiring her fire and her spirit and the way her shapely body moved as she marched away from him. He probably shouldn't have kissed her...but the temptation had been too strong and he had been right about the chemistry: she was dangerously provocative. It was a long time since a woman had intrigued him so much. OK, she was a loose cannon as far as his client was concerned, and totally untrustworthy...but what the hell? Why not enjoy a little playtime along the path to getting rid of her? She was a worthy adversary.

The light went out as Libby was halfway to her bedroom and she scrabbled her way blindly to her door. This was a bit like her life at the moment, she thought wryly. She felt totally lost where Marc Clayton was concerned. She knew he was playing games with her. Therefore she should find it easy to keep him at arm's length, so why did she keep kissing him back like that? And why was the experience so enjoyable? No one had ever kissed her like that before...turned her on with such ease before. He seemed to breach her defences with the ease of a high tide against a sand wall. It was scary. How could a man she didn't even like do that to her?

She found her bedroom door and practically fell inside. One thing for sure, she would not move out from this hotel...no matter what!

Libby stripped off and headed into the bathroom to stand under the shower. She tried to clear all thoughts of

Marc Clayton from her mind, but she kept remembering the feel of his lips against hers, his hands against her skin.

He was obviously a skilled womaniser, she told herself sharply. And if she gave in to his kind of charms she really would deserve to be badly burnt.

CHAPTER SIX

WHEN Libby finally got into bed she fell immediately asleep, and her dreams were a confused mix of her father as she had last seen him and then Marc.

One moment she was a child again, chasing after her dad, asking him not to leave. Then Marc stepped in. 'I'm afraid your father isn't coming back and he doesn't want to see you again, Libby,' he said sternly.

The words made her toss restlessly in the bed.

Then she was here in this hotel with Marc. 'But if you do as you are told, maybe I'll arrange a meeting for you.' He had a very determined look on his face as he said those words, yet his voice had a curiously husky edge to it. 'You play this by my rules, or not at all.' He reached out to take hold of her and she struggled to get away, but he was too strong. Then he was kissing her and the next moment they were in an unfamiliar bedroom with a four-poster bed and he was starting to undress her. 'I knew you'd come around to my way of thinking.' He whispered the words against her ear as she started to surrender willingly to his caresses.

His hands were warm against her body, and his caresses disturbingly tender.

Then suddenly he was pulling away and there was the loud bang of a door as he slammed it behind him.

There was to be no meeting with her father and, like Simon, he had gone without a backward glance.

Libby woke with a start and sat up in her bed, her heart thundering against her chest.

It took a moment to realise that the bang of the door had not just been in her dreams. There was someone outside in the corridor.

Then she remembered that she was in a hotel and that the sounds she could hear were other people leaving their rooms. Libby lay back against the pillows, her heart rate gradually slowing.

What strange dreams! She didn't know which bit had upset her most, the fact that she had given in to Marc's lovemaking...*that would never happen*...or the fact that even in her dreams her father didn't want to see her.

Just say he really didn't want to meet up with her? Just say he was cool and withdrawn and told her he didn't want any future contact...didn't want to rebuild bridges. The thought was like ice inside her; Libby didn't think she would be able to bear that. She didn't want to intrude on his life, but it would be nice just to know that he cared, even at a distance.

Trying to dismiss the dreams, she looked at her watch. It was almost seven in the morning.

She wished that her accommodation had included breakfast because she would have given anything for a cup of coffee and a croissant. Throwing back the covers, she got up and padded across to draw back the curtains. The sky was a cloudless baby-blue; it looked as if it was going to be a lovely day. Time to go out and find a café, she thought, feeling happier.

Donning pale denim shorts and a pink T-shirt, she left her room and sprinted for the lift as fast as her pink flip-flops would allow, making it just before the lights cut out. She was getting the hang of this, she thought with a smile as she pressed the button for the ground floor.

It was warm outside, and the pavements were quiet. She strolled along the back streets and before long turned a corner and found herself down in the old quarter of town. There was a newsagent's open and, remembering her brush with the press last night, she went inside to see if there was anything about her in the papers.

There were no English papers so she bought a local French one, thinking that she could at least flick through the pictures and try out her schoolgirl French.

Tucking it under her arm, she continued on until she reached a pavement café where the smell of freshly baked bread and ground coffee beans was too good to ignore.

Libby sat down and ordered a coffee and a croissant and then leaned back in her chair savouring the warmth of the morning and the relaxed ambience. There was no-where like France, she thought with a sigh; it was just so civilised.

For a while she watched the people walking by, noting how attractive and slender the Frenchwomen were and how elegantly dressed. Then, with a promise that she would start going back to the gym as soon as she got home, she opened her paper.

To her relief there were no embarrassing photos of her kissing Marc Clayton. There was a photo of her father, however. She struggled to make sense of the article, but she could really only understand one word and that was hospital!

A flash of apprehension ran through her. Was her father ill?

As the waiter came out to serve someone else Libby caught his attention. 'Do you speak English?' she asked hopefully.

'A little.' He nodded.

'I just wondered if you could tell me what this article says, please?' She pointed to the paper and the waiter leaned closer.

'It is about the actor, Carl Quinton. He has been involved in a bad accident.'

'Is he OK?' Libby felt cold with fear.

The waiter shrugged. 'It just says that he has been taken to a hospital in LA.'

'Thank you.' Somehow Libby kept calm and paid her bill, then she hurried back towards her hotel, her heart racing. Just say her father was dead? The thought made her feel sick inside. She remembered feeling like this before, when her mum had told her he was dead... remembered the grief and the torment of not knowing exactly what had happened to him. How poignant to think she was within a whisper of seeing him again...only to lose him again! She had never felt so helpless or so isolated. How was she going to find out about her dad?

From nowhere a rush of other memories went through her mind: her dad taking her to school on her first day...and waiting for her when she came out. She remembered he'd brought her a little bag of sweets. 'A little something to brighten my princess's day,' he'd said. Her eyes blurred with tears. She couldn't bear thinking that something had happened to him...that she had come so close to seeing him again only for a cruel twist of fate to take him away. She wished suddenly that she had Marc's telephone number.

Then as she rounded a corner she saw Marc's car parked outside her hotel and her heart raced with relief...with panic. What was he going to tell her?

She saw him coming out of the hotel. He was dressed in jeans and a plain white T-shirt and as she watched he glanced at his watch as if he was in a hurry. 'Marc!' She called over to him and he looked up.

'There you are! I was wondering where you'd got to.'

'Is my father OK?' She started to cross over to him.

'Libby, be careful,' he called.

But it was too late because she had already stepped out, completely forgetting the traffic was coming in a different direction. The next moment there was an almighty squeal of brakes as a car heading straight for her tried to stop.

For a moment the world seemed to move in slow motion as she tried to get out of the path of the car, lost her balance and fell onto the road, hitting her head with a crack against the tarmac. She looked up just as the car skidded to a halt a few inches from her.

Marc was beside her in an instant and she noticed that he looked visibly shaken. 'Are you OK?'

'Yes. I think so.' She allowed him to help her to her feet and pick up her handbag; only vaguely did she register the fact that now there was a heated exchange going on between him and the driver of the car.

'It was my fault, Marc,' she murmured, feeling shaken and very foolish.

'He was driving too fast.' Marc put an arm around her and helped her to the other side of the road. 'But what on earth were you thinking about? You could have been killed.'

'I know; it was stupid of me.' Libby tried to pull herself together. 'But I'm all right.'

'You scared the hell out of me.' His tone was so sincere and so gentle now that it caused goose-bumps over her skin. He put a hand under her chin and tipped her face up to his. 'You've cut your forehead.'

'Have I?' His touch and his tone were doing strange things to her emotions and she wanted to cry suddenly. 'I'm fine, really I am.'

'I think we should get you to a doctor.'

'There is no need.' Libby pulled away from him, then looked up at him, her eyes wide. 'Marc, is my dad OK?

I saw an article in the paper and it said he'd had an accident.'

'Yes, he's OK.' Marc's eyes raked over her, noting her extreme pallor, the over bright glitter of tears in her eyes.

'Are you sure?' Her voice wavered.

Marc nodded. 'I was speaking to him on the phone only this morning.'

A sweet flood of relief rushed through her. 'Thank God! I saw the paper and I couldn't understand it. I thought he might be dead.' Her voice was filled with the horror of that thought.

Marc frowned. Libby looked so genuinely distressed that it took him aback. Was this why she had been rushing across the road in such agitation?

'Come on, let's get you inside,' he murmured huskily. 'You need to attend to that wound.'

She didn't argue, her head was thumping and she felt a bit sick. 'Maybe I just need to lie down for a bit,' she said shakily.

'You know, I don't think that is a good idea. You've obviously hit your head quite hard; you could have concussion.' Marc led her into the hotel and stepped into the lift with her.

Libby was so distracted by his words that she didn't register the fact that he was coming upstairs with her. 'Do you think so?' She had to admit her head was very painful.

'Well, I'd like to take you to a doctor, just to be on the safe side.'

The lift doors opened on the fourth floor.

'No, Marc, I don't think that is necessary!'

'Well, we will see,' Marc continued smoothly as he took hold of her arm and led her out into the corridor. 'My instincts are telling me we should quickly pack up

your things and check you out of here, then I'll drive you
up to Casualty.'

The light clicked out, leaving them in total darkness.
She stumbled and Marc put a steadying arm around her
shoulder. The gesture brought home the fact that he was
upstairs with her, and suddenly she realised that surrep-
titiously he was probably trying to move her out of here
and into his house, probably using the hospital as an excuse to galvanise her!

'I'm not going to hospital. It's ridiculous. I've only
banged my head slightly.' But even as she said the words
Libby was all too aware that her head was thumping very
painfully.

'Well, we won't be able to tell how bad the wound is
until we've cleaned it up.' Marc's arm tightened around
her as she tried to pull away. 'How far down is your
room?'

'It's just here.' As she turned towards her door she half
stepped against Marc and for a moment found herself
awkwardly pressed in his arms. The moment of intimacy
in the darkness made her heart race; she was aware of the
delicious scent of his aftershave, the warmth of his body,
the touch of his hand against her back.

'Sorry.'

'That's OK.' His voice sounded velvety deep against
her ear.

She stepped hurriedly away. 'There was no need for
you to come up here, you know. I'll be fine now.' She
fumbled in her bag for her key card, and then struggled
to find the slot in the door to insert it.

'Here, let me help.' His hand was over hers, taking the
card. The touch of his skin made her senses swim.

It was a tremendous relief when the door opened and
they stepped into the sunny room.

'Thank you, Marc, you can go now.' She knew she sounded a bit like someone very imperial giving out orders, but she couldn't help herself.

Marc smiled. 'I'm not leaving here without you, Libby,' he said calmly. 'But let's see to your forehead first.' He reached out caught hold of her hand and led her into the *en suite* bathroom.

She was going to argue, but as she caught sight of her reflection in the mirror over the washbasin she decided maybe he was right. Her forehead was badly gashed at the side; no wonder her head was pounding.

Marc turned on the hot water and then turned her firmly around to face him. Libby felt a bit like a child being looked after against her will. Gently he brushed her hair back from her face and surveyed the damage under the bright overhead lights. He was looking at her so intently that she could almost feel his eyes on her skin and she felt acutely self-conscious. It was crazy: her head was hurting and she felt ill, but instead of thinking about that she was wishing instead that she had put some brighter lipstick on this morning, made more of an effort with her hair.

There was some cotton wool by her sponge bag and he took some out, ran it under the tap, and then gently swabbed the area around the wound. He was very gentle, but the hot water stung and she flinched.

'Stay still, Libby.' He put one hand on her arm and continued carefully. 'It isn't deep,' he murmured, 'but it's a nasty bump.'

Libby was trying to concentrate on something other than the gentle touch of his hand and his closeness, because it was having a very perturbing effect on her. 'I'll be OK now.' She tried to pull away, but he held her steady.

'Stop being such a baby,' he murmured, his eyes on her forehead as he finished what he was doing. 'There...' He released her.

'Thank you.' She stepped back from him hastily.

Their eyes met and for a moment there was a strange feeling of intimacy swirling between them.

He smiled at her gently. 'You're welcome.' Then he turned away from her to wash his hands under the running water. 'Have you got any antiseptic in there?' he asked, nodding towards the sponge bag on the window sill.

'Yes, Doctor.' She couldn't resist the jibe. He sounded so authoritative.

Marc's lips twisted in a smirk. 'Well, I suggest you apply some.'

She nodded. 'So how is my dad, Marc? What happened to him?'

'I'll tell you all about that later. In the meantime I suggest you pack up your things.'

'I've already told you I don't want to leave this hotel, Marc...' She started to make the protest but he wasn't listening, he had already walked out of the room before she had finished speaking.

Hell, but he was infuriating. She opened up her sponge bag, took out some antiseptic and dabbed it over the gash on her head. It didn't look too bad now that Marc had cleaned the wound.

'I suggest we get a move on, Libby,' Marc said from the bedroom.

She put the tube of cream away and headed through to the other room. 'Look, I appreciate your help to-day...but—' Libby came to a surprised halt as she saw that he had put her canvas bag on top of the bed and unzipped it. As she watched him he turned towards the wardrobe and started to take her clothes off the hangers to throw them into the bag.

'Marc!' Libby was horrified. 'I've told you I'm not leaving here. Now, will you please stop?'

He glanced over at her. 'I thought I made it clear last night that you are not in a position to argue about this.'

'I know what you said last night, but—'

'Well, then, you know that if you want me to help you get in touch with your dad you are going to have to take my advice and come with me now.' Calmly he continued to take the rest of her clothes off the hangers.

Libby bit down on her lip as fury mounted inside her. She hated to give in to his domineering bullying tactics... But what should she do? Marc was her only point of contact with her father.

As much as she hated to admit it...even to herself...she really didn't have a choice. If she wanted to speak to or see her dad, she was going to have to do as she was told. She certainly didn't want to feel the way she had a little while ago when she hadn't even known if he was alive or dead!

Marc had finished emptying her wardrobe and was turning towards the chest of drawers now.

'Excuse me! I'll take over from here, thank you.' She stepped in smartly before he could start taking the contents of her underwear drawer out.

'Well, get a move on.' Marc smiled to himself as he watched her empty the contents of her drawers into the bag. It looked as if he had won this round, he thought...but, hell, she was a tough cookie to break.

Libby was fizzing inside; she hated backing down. She glanced up and met his dark, watchful eyes. 'Don't feel too smug,' she told him pointedly. 'You've got twenty-four hours to arrange a meeting for me with my dad. And if you haven't done that, then I'm moving out of your safe house and back here.'

Marc shrugged. 'I'll see what I can do,' he said casually.

'You'll do more than that—'

'Libby,' he cut across her smoothly, 'just finish your packing.'

'Hateful…hateful man.' Libby went into the bathroom to get her sponge bag. As she zipped it up she glanced in the bathroom mirror at her reflection. Her head was spinning with the effort of arguing with Marc and her forehead looked red and sore again. She put her hand up to it and for a moment found herself remembering how tenderly Marc had bathed the wound…how concerned he had sounded.

Not that she was taken in by a bit of false sympathy. He'd only helped her up to her room so he could pack her bag. And she'd let him! Biting down on her lip, she reminded herself that going along with Marc's plans was a necessary evil.

'Are you ready?' When she went back through to the bedroom Marc was standing by the door with her bag in his hand.

'I think so.' Libby hurriedly had a last check around the room to make sure she had everything, before following him downstairs.

'I really don't know what the hurry is all about,' she murmured as they stepped out into the sunshine.

'The press might be sniffing around soon.' He opened the passenger door of his car for her before throwing her case in the boot. 'And, besides, you need to get that wound on your head checked out and I have other things to do today. I'm a busy man.'

'I probably do need my head testing,' she said dryly. 'I must be mad letting you move me out of my hotel.'

Marc smirked at that. 'For what it's worth I think you made the right decision.'

'I'm sure you do,' Libby muttered. 'And I don't really need a doctor. I'll be OK after a rest.'

She watched him put the car in gear and pull out into the flow of traffic away from the hotel. The feeling that she was making a very big mistake wouldn't go away... In fact, it was getting stronger with every moment that passed. A part of her wanted to tell him to stop the car so she could climb out.

She leaned her head back against the comfortable seat and tried to relax. Her headache seemed to be getting worse, but perhaps it was due to tension.

'So how is my father?' she asked tentatively.

'I told you. He's fine.'

'I know what you said,' Libby murmured. 'But do you think you could give me a little more detail? What happened to him exactly? Is he in hospital?'

Marc didn't answer her immediately; he seemed to be concentrating very hard on the traffic.

'Marc!'

'Your father is fine, Libby.' He flicked an impatient glance over at her. 'I don't know exactly what happened, but he's not in hospital. He's at his house in LA.'

'Oh! Well, that's good.'

Libby's voice sounded so heartfelt that Marc was struck once again by how genuinely concerned she seemed about her father. He frowned and told himself impatiently that she probably only cared because if anything happened to her father she might not get any of his money.

Then he glanced over at her again. Her head was relaxed back against the car seat and she had closed her eyes. He could see the wound at the side of her forehead quite clearly in the sunlight and it looked painful. In fact she looked very fragile, her beautiful skin completely ashen, her long dark lashes and glossy dark hair a stark contrast against the unnatural pallor. It was hard to believe that anyone who looked so defenceless and so beautiful could have a bad thought in her head.

He glanced back at the road and told himself not to be taken in by appearances. A few moments passed in silence.

'Libby, you're very quiet. Are you feeling OK?'

She didn't answer him.

'Libby?' He looked sharply over at her again and for one awful moment he wondered suddenly if she had passed out. 'Libby, are you OK?'

Her eyelashes flickered upwards briefly. 'Yes. Stop making a racket.'

Relieved by the normal antagonism in her tone, he had to smile. 'How's the head?'

'It hurts a little, but I'll be fine.' She closed her eyes again.

'You sound a bit sleepy?'

'I am a bit. Probably the aftermath of worrying about Dad.'

The signs for the hospital were coming up and Marc switched lanes to follow them. 'Maybe you had better not sleep until you've been checked over by a doctor.'

Libby opened her eyes. 'Marc, I've told you I don't need a doctor.'

'Just humour me, OK?'

'I think I'm humouring you enough moving to this safe house of yours,' she murmured.

'Even so, I'd feel better if you had a check-over. Don't

forget—if anything happens to you, I have your father to answer to.'

Would her dad really care? The question burned unpleasantly inside her and she closed her eyes against the harsh reality that maybe the answer to that would be no.

'Lib, don't go to sleep.' Marc reached out and touched her arm.

'I'm not asleep,' she said firmly.

The car came to a halt and she opened her eyes to find that they were outside a hospital. 'Marc, this is ridiculous! I don't really think we should waste a doctor's time on a small bump on the head.'

Marc ignored her totally and climbed out of the car. 'Come on, let's get you inside.' He came around to help her out.

She wanted to tell him that she didn't need the arm he put around her. But strangely it felt like too much effort to pull away. Hazily she couldn't help feeling that it was a shame Marc Clayton was such a ruthless bastard because when she closed her eyes and melted against him it felt good... His arms felt like a safe place to be.

Maybe she wasn't well if she was thinking like that! The thought gave her the strength to pull away from him. 'Marc, I'm fine.' But even as she said the words she did feel a little woozy.

Medical staff met them as they walked through the front door. Libby listened to the foreign voices and felt quite grateful that Marc was with her and able to deal with things.

'They have a doctor who speaks English, they are just getting him,' he told her.

'OK, thanks.'

Someone produced a wheelchair. 'I don't need that!' Libby murmured.

'Come on, don't be a difficult patient.'

'Marc!' She was going to argue with him, but she felt a bit dizzy, as if someone had swung her around on a dance floor under bright disco lights until everything was spinning around her. And suddenly the ground just seemed to fold under her and the last thing she remembered was Marc catching her and holding her close.

CHAPTER SEVEN

THEY were shining lights in her eyes again. Libby felt as if she had been prodded and poked enough. Although she was in a private room in the hospital and she couldn't fault the level of care, she still felt that one night in here was long enough.

'So do you think I can go home now, Doctor?'

'Will you be on your own?' The doctor spoke English with a delightful accent. If Libby hadn't been so anxious to leave she might have been tempted to just lean back against the pillows and listen to him all afternoon.

'I'm going to be staying in a villa for a few days and I think there will be staff there—why do you ask?'

'You have had mild concussion and really need to take it easy for a day or two. Also you need to make sure there is no recurrence of your symptoms. That means careful monitoring. If you have someone with you to watch over you it would be better.'

This made Libby frown. 'Well, I'm sure the staff will be there,' she said, trying to sound more positive. She really didn't want to spend another night in hospital.

There was a tap on the door and she looked over and saw Marc standing there a bouquet of beautiful flowers in his hands. 'Is it OK if I come in?' He looked from the doctor towards her and Libby felt very glad to see him.

'Yes, come in,' she said hurriedly.

He smiled at her and it was a smile that sent strange little butterflies dancing through her body.

There was no doubt about it: he was too damn handsome, she thought hazily. And he looked especially good this afternoon dressed casually in a pair of chinos and a cream shirt that sat easily on his broad-shouldered frame. He just seemed so powerfully sexy that he took her breath away.

'*Ça va, Marc?*' the doctor said jovially. The fact that he greeted Marc by name took Libby aback slightly.

Marc put the flowers down beside her on the bed stand.

'They are lovely, thank you,' Libby said, admiring the mix of pale peach roses and vivid blue irises.

'So how are you feeling?' Although Marc asked the question gently, his eyes seemed to burn through her in a way that made her feel very self-conscious. And suddenly she wished that she weren't lying in bed and that she were wearing something a little more stylish than this plain white hospital nightdress.

'I feel OK.' She shrugged. 'Ready to leave, in all honesty.'

'I was just explaining to Libby that I can discharge her, but I feel it would be best if she has someone close by to watch over her for the next twenty-four hours,' the doctor told Marc.

'Well, that is no problem,' he said swiftly. 'It goes without saying that I'll keep a close eye on her.'

'Good.' The doctor smiled at Libby. 'There, that is all settled. Now, if you experience a blackout or feel light-headed, abnormally drowsy or nauseous, I want you to seek medical assistance immediately.'

'Yes, of course.' Libby smiled weakly back. She was relieved to be leaving hospital, but the thought of Marc Clayton watching over her for twenty-four hours made her extremely edgy.

She darted a hesitant look up at him and he smiled.

'You will feel much better when you get out in the fresh air and get some sunshine on your skin.'

'Yes, I suppose I will, thank you.' Libby reassured herself that he was probably only pretending that he would keep an eye on her. Probably he would ask his cook or his cleaner at his house to stay over and check in on her. Not that she needed watching. Indeed she felt quite a fraud being detained in here overnight. She felt fine.

Marc accompanied the doctor out of the room and Libby noticed that they spoke in French as they left. She watched as they stood outside and continued to talk. What were they saying? she wondered. Marc was obviously asking questions about her health, and he looked concerned.

A nurse bustled in and smiled at her. '*Bonjour, mademoiselle.*'

'*Bonjour.*' Libby smiled back at her.

'I will help you get dressed ready to go home...yes?'

'Yes.' Libby nodded and wondered where home was going to be for the next few nights.

The door was closed and Marc was lost from sight. 'Your boyfriend is very handsome,' the nurse said with a grin as she brought Libby's things over for her.

Libby laughed. 'He's not my boyfriend. He's just...' She hesitated. What was Marc to her? 'He's...well, he's more a business associate.'

'I am surprised!' The nurse shrugged. 'We all thought that a romance was in the air. *Monsieur* Clayton was so concerned about you. He stayed here with you until very late last night.'

'Did he?' Libby was stunned at that piece of information; the time in hospital was all a bit of a blur to her.

'*Ah, oui.*' The nurse nodded. 'And he insisted that you

had the best private room…but then *Monsieur* Clayton is
a very caring man.'

'You seem to know him quite well.'

'Mm. Clayton spends a lot of time in France. He is a
friend of the doctor and very highly respected.' The nurse
grinned for a moment. 'And of course because he is so
good-looking and so high profile everyone is interested in
his romantic life.'

'Well, I can assure you there is no romance between
us,' Libby said emphatically. 'We hardly know each
other, in fact.'

The nurse looked disappointed. 'Ah, such a pity. We
all thought what a lovely couple you make and how he
obviously adores you because he was so concerned.'

For a moment Libby felt a warm glow of pleasure at
the words. Then she realised that Marc had probably just
been worried in case the press turned up and she said
something out of turn…That was more realistic.

It was strange, but the rational explanation brought with
it a very cold disappointment. Libby frowned. Maybe she
did have concussion! She knew all to well how little Marc
thought of her and his opinions were of no importance!
All that mattered was getting out of here and seeing her
dad, she reminded herself forcefully.

A little while later Libby was leaving the hospital. Marc
walked alongside her as they stepped through the front
doors, a helping hand under her arm. To Libby's surprise
they were met by a group of reporters and as cameras
clicked questions were fired.

'Can you tell us if there is any truth in the rumours that
Ms Sheridan is Carl Quinton's daughter?' someone called,
but Marc was hurrying her away, his arm protectively
shielding her from the intrusive glare of curiosity.

'Please, guys, give us a break,' he said curtly. 'Ms Sheridan really isn't up to this.'

'What about the rumours coming from the hospital that there is a romance brewing between the two of you?'

Marc made no reply to that as he helped her into the car.

'Well, I'm glad to get out of there,' Libby murmured once they were driving away.

Still Marc made no reply; he seemed to be lost in thought.

Libby studied his profile reflectively. He looked rather stern, she thought, and suddenly she wondered if he'd had the notion she had something to do with those romantic rumours at the hospital that the press had asked about. 'Look, in case you are wondering, I had absolutely nothing to do with starting those rumours at the hospital,' she told him heatedly. 'The nursing staff got the wrong idea because you seemed concerned about me. I mean…they weren't to know that you couldn't really give a toss if I lived or died and were just worried about the press getting to me.'

Marc was watching her with a puzzled frown between his eyes. 'Libby, I didn't for one moment think you had started any rumours at the hospital,' he said calmly. 'They are probably only asking because of those photos of us kissing the other day.'

'Oh!' Libby settled back against her seat and felt a bit foolish for getting so agitated now. 'Anyway, I scotched the rumour before I left the ward,' she murmured. 'I told the nurse you were just a business associate.'

'A business associate?' Marc sounded amused.

'Well, I had to say something,' she said emphatically. 'I didn't want that story going around either.'

'No, of course not.' He took his eyes off the road and

for a moment his gaze moved over her with gentle contemplation. 'You've got your reconciliation with your
boyfriend to think about, haven't you?'

Immediately she felt a flare of embarrassment as she
remembered how she had lied about that. 'Well...yes,'
she mumbled.

'And just for the record I did care about your welfare
at the hospital. In fact, I was extremely worried about
you.'

'Were you?' There it was again, that crazy, warm glow
of pleasure...He didn't mean it, she reminded herself
firmly.

He smiled at her. 'You gave me quite a scare, in fact.'

The warm glow suddenly became disturbingly intense.

'I think the only thing that truly concerns you is the
effect of negative publicity on my father's career,' she
said.

'Well, it goes without saying that I am apprehensive
about that,' he said with a shrug.

There, you see, she told herself resolutely. He really
doesn't give a damn about you. Now if only she could
maintain the same cool equilibrium around him, this situation might not feel so explosive.

She glanced over at him again. It was a pity he was so
good-looking; that was a definite distraction. To make
herself feel better she searched for faults. He looked very
autocratic, she told herself. His nose was slightly aquiline
and his mouth curved with a blatant sensuality. He wasn't
at all her type. But he was very attractive...a small voice
insisted.

As her eyes studied him she noticed that he still looked
extremely serious, almost as if something was troubling him.

'If you don't mind my saying so you look a bit...pensive,' she said distractedly. 'Is anything wrong?'

'No...nothing is wrong.' Marc glanced over at her again and gave her a reassuring smile.

Then he applied his attention firmly back to the road.

For some reason Libby didn't believe him. 'Are you sure?'

'Positive.' Marc's tone was brisk. He didn't want to tell her that in fact he had been deep in contemplation about a phone call he had made this morning to her father.

He'd rung to say that Libby was in hospital, but not to worry, she was OK, and he had half expected Carl to want to dash to her bedside, had been prepared with calming words to stop him worrying, but Carl had made no such panicky suggestion. All he'd said was that he was glad she was making a full recovery.

It was a bit of a surprise...but then not everyone reacted to a crisis in the same way. Maybe Carl had been trying to play down the fact that he was really desperately worried about his daughter.

'My dad is well, isn't he?' Libby asked suddenly. 'You're not keeping anything from me, are you?'

Marc glanced over at her with a frown. She sounded more concerned about her father than he had about her. It was a puzzle.

'Yes, he's fine,' he murmured distractedly, and looked back at the road.

'He is still coming to the film festival?'

Marc glanced over at her again and she smiled hopefully, her blue eyes wide with anticipation.

She is just a good actor, he reminded himself firmly. 'Yes, he will be arriving in a few days.'

'A few days.' The excitement faded in her eyes. 'I thought he would arrive earlier than that. Didn't you say something in your email about him arriving two days after me?'

'Yes, well, there has been a change of plan.'

'Oh…I see!' Libby tried not to feel disappointed and told herself that the only thing that mattered was that she saw him before she had to return to London. But the dull ache inside refused to go away. She wondered if Marc was responsible for the delay in her father getting here.

Marc glanced over at her and noticed the way the light seemed to have faded from her expression.

'You'll enjoy a few days being pampered at the villa,' he told her cheerfully. 'It's just what the doctor ordered.'

She smiled, but it lacked her usual sparkle.

'And tomorrow we could go for lunch into Nice, if you'd like?' He found himself impulsively issuing the invitation.

'Why?' She looked over at him suspiciously.

He laughed. 'Do we have to have a reason to have lunch?'

She shrugged. 'I thought you wanted to keep me tucked up in this safe house of yours, away from the prying eyes of reporters and anyone else with a passing interest?'

'Lunch in Nice will be OK. Most of the press interest will be centred in Cannes.'

'Yes, well, I think I'll pass, thanks,' she said moodily.

He looked over at her with a frown. 'Why?'

'Because having lunch with someone who thinks so badly of me doesn't sound like much fun anyway.'

'I see.' Marc's voice seemed to take on a harder edge. 'Well, if you change your mind the offer still stands.'

'I won't change my mind,' she said firmly. Libby tried to concentrate on the scenery and not on the sudden tense atmosphere in the car. The view was spectacular. They were travelling along a narrow winding road that hugged the side of a cliff. The rock face was a dazzling red against a blue sky and the vivid turquoise of the sea. Every now and then she glimpsed secluded coves where people lay in the sun and swam in the warmth of the Mediterranean. Libby wished that she were down on one of those beaches with nothing to worry about other than which sun factor to wear.

Marc turned the car up into a private drive and stopped to allow imposing wrought-iron gates to swing open automatically. The car swept through and they closed smoothly behind them as they continued up a long tree-lined drive.

'That's my prison perimeter, is it?' Libby half joked.

He flicked a wry look over at her. 'You can come and go as you like,' he said. 'I told you that. You will have Jacques to drive you.'

'I can drive myself, you know,' she murmured. 'And I don't need a spy out with me watching my every move.'

'Jacques is a chauffeur, Libby, not a spy. And I'd let you have a car, but that would involve getting you insured. It's easier just to use my driver.'

It sounded so practical that Libby almost felt convinced...almost but not quite. She knew all too well that she was only here because Marc wanted to keep a close eye on her. Of course the chauffeur would be a spy...it stood to reason.

The drive widened out into a courtyard and in front of them was a large and impressive provincial villa. It had a red-tiled roof and its pale blue walls were covered in a riot of bougainvillea and wisteria. Curved stone steps led up to a glossy dark blue front door.

'Do you own this place?' Libby was impressed.

'Yes. Do you like it?'

'It's beautiful...but more like a mansion than a villa.'

Mark smiled. 'I have some staff who live in; Marion the housekeeper and her husband Claude, who looks after the garden. They occupy the side annexe of the house.'

'And you keep the place just for clients who need space and security?'

'Yes.' He pulled to a halt by the front door and she picked up her handbag and the bouquet of flowers Marc had brought for her before turning and allowing him to help her out of the car.

Money was obviously no object to Marc Clayton, she thought as they walked into a very grand entrance hall with a sweeping staircase, polished wood floors and modern chandeliers.

She wondered what his house next door would be like if this was just an auxiliary residence.

'Now, the doctor has given me strict instructions that you have to take things easy,' Mark said as he tossed some keys down onto the hall table. 'So what I suggest is that, after you've settled in, we sit and have a drink in the garden before having dinner.'

'Don't you have to get back to your own house?' Libby asked politely. 'I know what a busy man you are—you must have a million things to do.'

Marc decided it best to ignore the note of sarcasm in her tone. 'No, I've cleared my calendar just for you,' he said, matching her tone exactly.

'Ah, and here's Marion now.'' Marc smiled as a woman of about sixty, wearing an attractive flower-print dress, appeared from the back of the house. 'Perhaps you'd be good enough to show Libby up to her room, Marion. I just need to make a few phone calls.'

Marion smiled at her as she led the way upstairs. 'We were sorry to hear about your accident, *mademoiselle*. How are you feeling now?'

'Much better, thank you.' Libby glanced around and saw Marc disappearing into a study off the hallway.

Marion led her up onto a wide landing and opened the first door for her.

Libby walked into a lovely room with pale lilac walls and windows that looked out towards the sea. But it was the bed that took her attention and the fact that it was a king-sized four-poster romantically draped with white muslin.

Suddenly out of nowhere she remembered her dream from the other night when Mark had taken her into his arms and made love to her.

Her heart missed a beat and thudded violently against her chest at the vivid and disturbingly intense image. She remembered the way she had surrendered to him so easily...and, most disquieting, the way he had told her if she did as she was told he would arrange a meeting for her with her father...a promise he had subsequently not fulfilled.

'Shall I take these flowers for you and put them in some water?' Marion leaned across and took the bouquet from her. The gesture snapped her out of her reverie. That had just been a stupid dream; it was crazy to even give it a second thought, she told herself sternly.

'There is an *en suite* bathroom through there,' Marion continued with a wave towards a door at one end of the room.

'Thank you.'

'I'll arrange for your bag to be brought up.'

Marion left the room and Libby wandered through to the bathroom. It was fitted out in white and gold and was very luxurious.

She glanced at her reflection in the mirrored walls. She looked very pale and her forehead still looked inflamed at one side. She decided to take a shower and wash the hospital feeling away. And then maybe Marc was right and a quiet spell in the garden would make her feel back to normal.

There was a tap on the bedroom door and when Libby went through to investigate she saw her bag had been brought up for her.

Quickly she unpacked her things. She wished she had brought more clothes with her now. This house and this situation seemed to call for something a little more glamorous than a couple of summer dresses.

With a sigh she closed the drawers and went to shower and change.

When Libby went back downstairs she could see Marc was still in the study talking on the telephone. So she left him and wandered down the hallway until she found the sitting room. It was a very elegant room with primrose carpets and pale blue chairs. Although there was a sense of opulence about the décor, there were also pretty touches like the traditional provincial print of the cushions and the curtains and the enormous stone fireplace that was so large you could have sat inside it by the fire.

Libby glanced out of French windows that led towards a well-manicured garden. A swimming pool sparkled invitingly in the sun and beyond it the Mediterranean. Libby tried the doors, but they were locked. She turned and wondered if she should tell Marc that she was downstairs and then on second thoughts she just sat in one of the comfortable armchairs and decided to wait until he had finished his calls.

There was a remote control for the TV beside her and she flicked it on. The first couple of channels were in French, so she kept flicking until she reached an English-speaking station.

'And now for that latest update on Carl Quinton's accident.' An American newscaster with perfectly styled blonde hair smiled cheerfully. 'The actor was lucky to escape with just a few cuts and bruises when he was involved in a car crash in LA.'

A picture of a mangled car flashed onto the screen, a picture that horrified Libby.

'Friends close to the actor say that he is in good spirits and looking forward to the Cannes Film Festival where—'

Libby looked up as Marc walked into the room. 'You didn't tell me my father had been involved in such a bad car crash,' she murmured shakily. 'You said it was nothing!'

Marc picked up the remote control and switched the TV off. 'It was a publicity stunt, Libby,' he said, cutting across the anxious questions that were poised on her lips. 'There was no car crash, just an elaborate set-up for the press to get their teeth into.'

'I see.' She was thankful that her father hadn't been in that car! But after the initial relief a feeling of annoyance took her over. Marc should have told her the truth about the situation. 'And I take it this publicity stunt was planned well in advance?'

'No, actually, it was a last-minute decision.'

'But you knew about it when you took me out for dinner the other night?'

Marc hesitated momentarily and then inclined his head. 'Yes, I knew.'

'So why didn't you tell me?' She got to her feet and glared at him. 'Do you realise just how worried I was when I saw that newspaper report? You could have saved me that at least!'

His eyes flicked over her. She was wearing the blue summery dress she had worn on the evening they went for dinner. She looked lovely…she also looked delicate and very pale. And behind the anger in her blue eyes he imagined he could see a shimmer of unbearable sadness.

'I'm sorry, Libby, really, I had no intention of causing you anxiety.'

The deep strength of his tone did nothing to assuage the hurt inside her. 'Sorry really just doesn't cut it,' she said shakily. 'Have you any idea what it is like to be separated from someone you once loved? To have them walk out of your life without any explanation and never see them again?' Her voice held a tremor of deep emotion.

Marc frowned. 'But you could have seen him again if you had wanted to,' he reminded her gently.

'Oh, yes, sorry, silly me. I forgot! I'm just some un-feeling, money-grabbing…harlot, aren't I?'

His lips twisted wryly at that. 'I never said you were a harlot.'

'You've never said anything nice about me either.' She flared. 'I suppose you didn't tell me the truth because you were afraid I'd let it slip to the press that it was just a publicity stunt?'

'That did cross my mind.' He shrugged.

For some reason that calm admittance hurt as well.

'Hey.' He reached out and gently touched her face. 'I am sorry. I really didn't mean to upset you. I'd hoped to pick you up from your hotel before the news about your father broke. Then I could have reassured you myself. I was a bit surprised to find you weren't in the hotel when I arrived.'

The touch of his hand was very disconcerting, as was the gentleness of his tone. She stepped quickly away from him. 'Those are just excuses, Marc. The fact is you delib-erately keep me in the dark.'

Marc felt a tinge of guilt. Maybe if he had told her the

truth about that PR stunt she wouldn't have stepped out
in front of that car. How genuine was her concern about
her father? he wondered. Had he got it wrong? Or was
she just damn good at playing make-believe?

Marion came in at that moment with a tray in her hand.
'I brought you some iced tea.' She smiled at Marc.
'Would you like it in here or out in the garden?'

'In the garden, *merci,* Marion,' Marc replied.

As the woman unlocked the French doors and disappeared outside Marc raked a hand distractedly through his
hair. No matter what the truth of the situation, he did
know one thing for certain and that was how fragile and
vulnerable Libby had looked in that hospital bed. 'Look
Libby, you shouldn't really be upsetting yourself like this.
Dr Lavelle said that you should take things easy, avoid
stress. So what do you say we call a truce? I am genuinely
sorry that I didn't tell you about the publicity stunt…and
you have my word that I won't keep you in the dark about
anything like that again, and I promise I will arrange a
meeting for you with your father.'

'Really?' Libby looked up at him warily. 'You promise?'

He nodded and reached out to take hold of her arm.
'Come on, let's go and sit outside and relax.'

Libby hesitated for a moment. The look in his eyes had
been so solemn, but could she really trust him to follow
through with that guarantee?

They walked out through French windows into the garden. There was a spectacular view over the Mediterranean.
Little white sailing boats were flecked over the horizon and
the jagged coastline stretched for miles, thickly wooded with
no other houses in sight. The trees evidently screened Marc's
place, but a narrow twisty path led down through the green-
ery to a secluded private cove just below them. She remem-

bered Marc telling her the beach connected the two prop-
erties.

'This is some place,' Libby marvelled as she walked
with him towards the table and chairs by the pool.

'Yes, eventually I'd like to live out here in France full
time.' He pulled a lounger around for her so that she was
under the shade of the parasol and could relax and look
out to sea.

'But what about your little girl? You wouldn't leave
her, would you?'

'No.' Marc shook his head. 'That would be unthinka-
ble. But I have some plans that could allow me the best
of both worlds.'

'What kind of plans?' she asked curiously.

He smiled. 'Being on the superstitious side, I'd rather
not say at the moment. Let's just leave it that I shall be
putting my proposal into action during the Cannes Film
Festival.'

'Sounds intriguing.' Libby couldn't help wondering if
the real reason he wasn't telling her his plans was down
to the fact that he didn't trust her with them. Well, she
didn't trust him either, she told herself firmly as she ad-
justed the chair and sat down, hitching her skirt up just a
little to let the sun at her legs.

'What about you?' Marc asked suddenly. 'Do you like
living in London?'

'It's OK. Feels a bit like being in a rat race sometimes,
but it has its compensations. There are good shops, good
theatres and it's a cosmopolitan way of life.'

'You are in advertising, I believe?'

'Yes.' She looked over at him with a raised eyebrow.
'But you already know all there is to know about me,
don't you? Or rather you think you do, courtesy of your
private detective?'

He smiled. 'Now, that is not true at all. I only asked him to check you out to make sure you were who you said you were.'

'Plus a little financial assessment on the side.' Libby couldn't keep the dry tone out of her voice. 'Oh, and a little peek around in my private life as well.'

Marc shrugged. 'You can't blame me for being curious.'

Libby opened one eye and looked at him. 'Yes, I can, actually.'

He gave a wry smile. 'If it's any consolation, I was completely fascinated by you from the moment I saw your photograph.' The words were said in a warmly sensual tone. 'And there is a lot more that I would like to find out about you.'

To Libby's dismay she found her body responding quite fiercely to those words. Heat started to sizzle through her and she felt a sense of heightened awareness as their eyes connected.

With difficulty she pulled herself together. 'Now, Marc, I know that your laid-back flattery probably charms most women, but it doesn't work on me,' she told him briskly.

'Doesn't it?' He leaned a little closer. 'Are you sure?' he asked with a lazy kind of amusement that in itself made her heart beat faster.

'Of course I'm sure,' she murmured. 'Because I recognise your type and I know exactly what you are thinking.'

'And what is my type?' he asked, as if held spellbound by her every word. He leaned even closer.

'Well, you are…' She could hardly think straight with him so close. Even the scent of his aftershave seemed to disturb her senses. 'You're probably totally unprincipled.

You think that the right words and the right…look will get you exactly what you want.'

'As bad as that, eh?'

The amusement in his tone was most disconcerting. She glanced over at him with apprehension and noticed the way his eyes flicked down over her curvaceous body and long, shapely legs.

'So, do you know what I'm thinking now?' His voice lowered to a husky drawl.

Libby was suddenly acutely aware that behind the light-hearted bantering lay a much more intense feeling of sexual magnetism. She could feel it like a physical presence swirling between them, and for some reason the emotions scared her. She could so easily lose herself in him, she thought hazily as she stared into the darkness of his eyes. Hastily she looked away.

'Yes…you are thinking that I'm a pushover,' she said abruptly. 'And, I can assure you, I'm not.'

He laughed at that. It was most unfair, she thought grimly, because even his laugh was attractive.

'I never for one moment thought that about you, Libby.'

'Good.' She glanced back at him and couldn't help but smile as she met his gaze. 'As long as we understand each other,' she murmured.

'Oh, I think we understand each other perfectly.' His gaze moved towards her lips.

Something about the way he was looking at her made her tremble inside…made her want to lean closer across the small gap between them and kiss him…melt against him and forget everything else…

Hurriedly she glanced away from him and moved the conversation on, saying the first thing that came into her mind. 'You know, I hope you don't feel you have to stay

around here with me because of what the doctor said. I'll
be perfectly OK on my own, if you'd like to go.'

He didn't answer her immediately and when she looked
back at him she noticed there was a serious expression in
his dark eyes now. 'I gave my word to the doctor that I
would watch over you, and I have no intention of leaving
you, Libby.'

'But I am fine…really I am.'

'Even so.' He smiled at her. 'I'm afraid you are stuck
with me for the evening.'

He reached to pour her a drink from the table at the
other side of him. The only sounds in the garden were the
soft clink of ice cubes against glass, and the drone of a
bee as it plundered the heavy head of a pink climbing
rose. It was a perfectly tranquil scene and yet Libby could
feel the danger in her situation swirling around her.

She was sexually attracted to Marc. No matter how she
tried to deny it, there was a certain chemistry between
them that wouldn't go away. And even more troubling
was the fact that she was sure Marc was just as aware of
it as she was.

CHAPTER EIGHT

As MARC handed Libby the glass of iced tea he noticed how carefully she accepted it, as if she wanted to avoid any contact with him.

The silence between them was heavy.

Libby sought around for something to say to break the feeling of tension. 'This drink is very refreshing.'

'Yes, it's Marion's own special recipe. She is an absolute gem.'

'Unfortunately I haven't got very good culinary skills.' Libby knew she was talking rubbish now; it was something she did when she felt nervous.

'Well, you probably have other more important talents than cooking, Libby,' he said smoothly.

She didn't dare look over at him; the low, sexy quality to his tone was enough to tell her they had by no means skated onto safer ground.

Instead she watched the sun as it started to go down leaving a shimmer of pink over the tranquil dove-blue sea. The evening was drawing in fast now and lights started to turn on in the garden. They twinkled in the purple light of dusk along the edges of the flowerbeds and highlighted the pool in fluorescent turquoise.

Libby darted a glance over at Marc and found he was watching her almost as closely as she had been watching the sunset. It made her feel acutely self-conscious. She didn't know if she was glad of the velvety darkness that was starting to surround them, or more perturbed by its intimacy.

'So, tell me, Marc, what is my dad like these days?' she asked, trying to put her mind to more important things.

'He's a really nice guy,' Marc said cautiously.

'Tell me a little bit about him.'

Marc hesitated. 'I suppose you know that, counting your mother, he has been married three times?'

'Yes, I had heard. He doesn't seem to have much luck in love, does he?' Libby reflected. 'It's strange that he hasn't had more children.'

'Not really. I think losing you cut him up pretty badly.'

Libby wondered how true that was.

'Apart from that there is not much to tell,' Marc continued. 'He lives in LA and he had a moderately successful career in local TV there. That was where I discovered him and from that point things really took off for him in a big way.'

Libby smiled at that. 'You are nothing if not modest, Marc.'

'I'm just telling you what happened.' He shrugged. 'Carl didn't have proper representation, but he did have a lot of talent. I, on the other hand, have the business acumen and the contacts; I saw the possibilities, stepped in and signed him. Since then his career has been in sharp ascendancy in the States. And now he's starring in a film with Julia Hynes who as you know is very much on the A list when it comes to celebrities. So I think you could say he really has made the big time now.'

As Marc was speaking she could see the glint of achievement in his eyes. 'You obviously love the cut and thrust of business,' she murmured. 'But it's quite a ruthless industry, isn't it?'

'It can be.' Marc finished his drink.

'Is that why you like it?' she asked impulsively.

He glanced over at her and for a moment their eyes held. 'Well, put it this way, I have never backed away from a challenge,' he said quietly.

A little shiver raced down Libby's spine. Going head to head against Marc was a risky business. She supposed she had known that from the first moment she'd met him at the airport. He was a man who got what he wanted and wasn't afraid to play rough if circumstances demanded it. So, knowing how ruthless he was prepared to be…why was she so attracted to him? she wondered dazedly. Was it the sense of danger that was turning her on?

'I think you are the same,' Marc said suddenly. 'I think you also don't like to back away from a challenge.'

'Maybe…' She admitted the fact almost under her breath.

'And maybe that is why there is a certain chemistry between us,' Marc reflected softly.

'Is there?' She moistened her lips nervously and wondered how they had managed to slide onto such dangerous ground so suddenly.

'You know there is.' His eyes were on her lips now and she could feel her heart thundering against her chest.

She was very glad that Marion chose that moment to step out of the house and announce that dinner was ready.

'Saved by the bell,' Marc reflected wryly.

'I don't need saving, Marc.' She batted wide blue eyes up at him, and ignored the hand he held out to help her up.

His lips twisted wryly. 'If you say so,' he murmured. 'But I think time will tell.'

Libby lay in the deep comfort of the four-poster bed, but she couldn't sleep. Not only was she unbearably hot, but also her mind kept replaying back over the evening.

She had to admit that it had been delightful sitting in Marc's dining room with the candlelight flickering on the table between them. The food had been delicious and Marc had been good company. Somehow the conversation had been steered away from any kind of dangerous ground for most of the night and they had even managed to laugh together about some silly inconsequential matters.

She sensed now that it had been Marc who had done the steering. He had cleverly drawn her out and she had said a few things she hadn't meant to. For one, she had admitted that her credit card bills were out of hand...

That had been a big mistake; as soon as she'd said it she'd wanted to bite her tongue out. But Marc had led the conversation to that point...she realised that now. She tried to tell herself it didn't matter...after all, Marc already knew she was in financial trouble from his report on her and she hadn't answered his question about why she was in so much debt.

She tossed restlessly and then got up to open the bedroom window. There was a heavenly smell of lavender outside and the sky was clear and filled with a million stars. For a while Libby just leaned against the window sill and looked out. Moonlight reflected in the swimming pool and glistened over the darkness of the sea.

It was a very romantic setting, only the gentle tropical sound of cicadas to fill the warmth of the night. Libby suddenly remembered the way Marc had touched her hand lightly across the table as he'd made a point about something trivial. It had just been an insignificant fleeting moment, but it had set Libby's body completely on fire.

Had he done it on purpose? she wondered now. Had he been testing her, gauging her reaction...like a predator observing his prey's weakness?

Annoyed by the thought, she hurried back to bed. She was being ridiculous, imagining things.

Yet even so the undercurrent of tension inside her refused to go away, refused to allow her to sleep.

She tried to think about other things, but her mind kept returning to Marc.

It had been very clear just how much he adored his daughter; his love for the little girl had shone through in some of the things he had said about her and Libby had been entranced. It had made her like him more...made her relax.

'It's good that you are there for Alice,' she had told him impulsively. 'Divorce can be hard on children. I know I was unhappy for a long time after my parents split up.'

'Your mother remarried, though, didn't she?'

Libby nodded. 'But it was not the same. My stepfather was...' As soon as she started to tell him about Sean she realised her mistake. The information was simply too personal, and she hadn't meant to reveal anything like that to him.

'Was what?' he probed gently.

But by then thankfully she had withdrawn from the brink. Opening up and revealing painful memories to your enemy was not a good idea. She needed to keep strong around Marc Clayton...every instinct told her that. And, besides, out of respect for her mother she really didn't think she should talk about how volatile things had been in her mother's relationship.

'He was OK,' she said instead.

As their eyes met Libby had the distinct impression that Marc knew she was airbrushing things out.

She glanced at her watch then. 'I suppose it is getting rather late.'

'Is it?' He also looked at the time. 'It's only ten-thirty.'

'Yes, but I should turn in.' She smiled across at him. 'And I'm sure you'll want to get back to your own house. You've probably got a million things to do tomorrow. The film festival must be a busy time for you.'

'Yes, it is. But things won't really heat up until the day after tomorrow. I suppose you could say this is the calm before the storm. This week I have a few premières to attend and a lot of business meetings.'

'What day will *Family Values* première?'

'Wednesday...I think.'

'You think?' Libby looked at him with a raised eyebrow.

'Your father isn't my only client, Libby.'

'No...of course not.'

Even so she sensed he was prevaricating. She was sure Marc Clayton knew exactly what dates his clients' films were showing.

That thought gave her the impetus to stand up from the table. 'Well, thank you for a lovely evening,' she said politely.

'My pleasure.' He also got to his feet. 'I've enjoyed your company.'

He walked with her from the room and stopped by the bottom of the stairs. 'Well, thanks again,' she said, feeling awkward for some reason.

'Libby.' He caught hold of her arm as she made to turn away and then, to her surprise, bent to kiss her cheek.

The momentary contact was tantalisingly provocative. Libby longed to turn her head and meet his lips. It took all her will-power to turn away from him and wish him a cool goodnight.

Thinking about that moment now made her temperature rise further. She tossed restlessly. The thing that really irritated her was that she knew exactly what kind of man Marc Clayton was and yet she still felt drawn to him…like a lemming to a cliff.

She threw the sheets back, and gave up the pretence of trying to sleep. There was no way she could lie in this bed a moment longer, she was too filled with restless energy.

Libby wandered over to the window again and looked down at the darkness of the garden and the deserted terraces around the pool. She wondered suddenly if the water in that pool would be warm. Maybe a swim was just what she needed.

Impulsively she went over to the chest of drawers, took out her bathing suit and slipped it on. Then she put on her robe, took a towel and crept downstairs.

The house was in total darkness and she switched on a few lamps as she walked into the drawing room. Then she tried the French doors, half expecting them to be locked, but to her surprise they swung open easily.

The air outside was warm, and, although all the garden lights were switched off and the lawns and borders were in shadow, the pool was lit by the fullness of the moon.

Libby bent down and tested the water with her hand. It wasn't very warm. For a moment she contemplated going back to bed; only the thought of lying awake for another few hours stopped her.

She was out here now, so she might as well make the most of it. Without giving herself time to change her mind, she slipped off her robe and walked down the steps.

The water enveloped her in its dark, silky folds and for a moment it felt freezing against her skin, but as she started to swim her temperature increased and by the time she had reached the opposite side the water felt suddenly warm.

She swam several lengths, enjoying the exercise. Then she allowed herself to drift, looking up at the clear star-studded sky until the chill of the water started to bite again and she decided to get out. It was only as she turned to swim over to the steps that Libby suddenly realised that she was not alone.

Marc was sitting on one of the chairs on the patio.

'How long have you been there?' she asked in surprise.

'Quite a while,' he said lazily. 'I didn't feel tired so I came out here to get some fresh air.'

'I thought you had gone home ages ago.' She pushed her wet hair out of her eyes and clung to the side of the pool, reticent about climbing out now that she knew he was watching.

'Well, I'm glad I didn't. I wouldn't have liked to think you were out here alone after just getting out of hospital,' he said sternly.

'I'm fine, Marc.'

'That is a matter of opinion. If you had a blackout while in the water you could drown.' He stood up from the chair and as he walked closer she could see that he was still wearing the same clothes from dinner. Obviously he hadn't been home.

'I'm not going to black out. And there is no need to fuss.'

'All the same, I promised Dr Lavelle that I'd keep an eye on you.' He picked up her robe from the floor. 'Come on, you'd better get out of there before you catch a chill.'

'I'm not cold.' She really didn't want to step out of the water in front of him. Her swimming costume was very brief and she felt incredibly self-conscious. 'And I absolve you from the responsibility of watching over me,' she said with a grin.

He crouched down beside her. 'If you are not cold, how come you are shivering?'

The amusement in his tone really irritated her. 'I'm not,' she said firmly and tried very hard to stop her teeth from chattering. 'And I'll get out in a minute once you've gone.'

He smiled. 'I tell you what, I'll do the gentlemanly thing and turn my back while you get out and put your robe on, OK?'

Libby hesitated. 'Yes...OK, thanks.' She did need to get out of here. Now she had stopped swimming it was very cold.

He straightened and turned his back on her. But it was only as she got out of the water and looked around for her wrap that she realised he was still holding it. 'Marc, you've got my robe!'

'So I have.' He turned around and for a second his eyes drifted down over her figure. 'I don't know why you were hiding from me. You have a beautiful body...very shapely.'

The huskiness of his tone caused the shivers inside her to increase dramatically. 'Just cut the smooth talk, Marc, and give me my robe.' She held her hand out impatiently.

Instead of handing it to her, he came over and wrapped it around her shoulders. 'There, that's better.'

He was so close to her that she could feel the warmth from his body.

She wanted to step back from him, but she was too close to the edge of the pool. 'I suppose you thought that was funny?' She glared at him as she rubbed herself dry with the robe.

'What was funny?'

'Pretending to be a gentleman!'

'I thought I'd behaved impeccably,' he said.

'Well, I beg to differ.'

'Do you?' He reached out and touched her face. His hand caressed silkily over her wet skin and made her start to shiver again…for all the wrong reasons.

'I was very well behaved at dinner…didn't make a single pass at you and, believe me, I was extremely tempted.'

'Were you?' She looked up into his eyes and could feel her heart thumping against her chest violently.

He nodded. 'And then I wished you goodnight with just the lightest peck on the cheek when in fact what I really wanted to do was this…' He leaned closer and she realised he was going to kiss her, but she couldn't make herself move away.

His lips were warm against the coolness of hers; the feeling was extremely sensual, the kiss mind-blowing. She was reeling with the aftermath of it as he pulled back to look into her eyes. 'I let you walk away from me up the stairs, when really what I wanted to do was sweep you up into my arms and take you to bed.'

The softly spoken words caused an intense rush of consternation mixed with excitement. The truth was she had wanted that too, she still did. And that was what was scaring the hell out of her.

'So, you see, I think I've been very restrained,' he murmured huskily. 'I came out here to cool down…and then I saw this vision of loveliness disrobing to reveal tantalising curves. It really was very distracting and all my good intentions seem to be deserting me.'

'I didn't know you were here.' She whispered the words unsteadily.

'But maybe deep down you were hoping I was?' He traced a finger down the side of her face, and then lower to where the trim of her bathing suit curved around her feminine form.

'You are very sure of yourself, Marc Clayton,' she said. 'I have to tell you I don't even like you very much…'

'Don't you?' His fingers stroked lower over the wet costume and he could feel the hard peaks of her breasts. 'Your body begs to differ.'

'I'm cold,' she murmured, trying very hard to fight the melting fires inside.

'No, Libby…at this moment, I'd say you are very…very hot.' His mouth found hers again and this time the kiss was hungry and intense. She felt the last little glimmers of resistance fading under the masterful strokes of his hand and his mouth. And suddenly she was giving in completely to the desire that he could stoke inside her with such ease.

Her hands tentatively reached out to touch his shoulders, and then seemed to travel of their own volition to rake through his hair as she kissed him hungrily back.

She felt the straps of her bathing suit come loose as he untied them, felt him slowly pulling it down as his lips moved down over her neck and then lower. Libby was completely powerless to resist.

His thumb brushed over the sensitised peak of her breast before the warmth of his mouth covered it, and she caught her breath at the pure ecstasy of the sensation.

Then suddenly he was pulling her robe closed. A sharp dart of disappointment seared through her. Was he putting a stop to things?

As he stepped back from her she looked up into his eyes and realised she had passed the point of turning back. The ache inside her was too insistent to ignore.

He stroked her wet hair back from her face. The gesture was curiously tender and it made her stomach turn over with desire.

'Shall we go upstairs, make ourselves more comfortable?' he suggested softly.

A tense silence twisted between them.

Libby hesitated, torn between the weight of her desire and the ignobility of inviting a man who had no regard for her—indeed, thought she was nothing but a gold-digger—into her bed. If she slept with him this would just be sex; there would be no tender feelings attached. She had never done that in her life before.

She shivered violently and Marc pulled the robe closer around her. 'Let me help you get out of those wet things,' he murmured playfully and leaned closer to kiss her again.

His kiss was so seductively passionate it was hard to remember that this was just a fling.

Libby kissed him back tentatively, and suddenly the caress deepened, sensuality heightened and she forgot her misgivings...forgot everything except the raw, primal need that was racing between them.

'OK, you can take me to bed,' she whispered against his lips. 'Just this once...but it doesn't mean anything...'

Even as she was speaking he was swinging her up into his arms.

CHAPTER NINE

LIBBY stared up at the ceiling and watched shadowy early-morning sunlight creep in across the room.

She felt shell-shocked, could hardly believe that she had given herself so completely to Marc Clayton last night! But if she turned her head a fraction of an inch on the pillow, there he was next to her. She had slept with the enemy! And, what was worse, it had been absolutely fantastic!

Groaning inwardly, she tried not to think about how wonderful it had been. But the memories were vividly fresh in her mind. She remembered when Marc had brought her up to the bedroom she had disappeared into the bathroom to quickly shower the chlorine from her skin. It had been an excuse to escape for a moment, to try and pull back from the brink of disaster. But as the steaming water had hit her body the shower door had opened and Marc had joined her. She would never, ever forget the way he had turned her on, the feel of his hands so confident and so skilled in the art of seduction, his mouth plundering against hers, the power of his body against hers. Her stomach turned over with latent desire at the very thought of it.

Marc had awoken a deep and passionate sensuality in her that she hadn't even known existed until now. Nobody had ever made her lose control like that before...not even Simon, and yet she had thought she had loved Simon with all her heart! It was bizarre that a man like Marc—a man whom she really didn't like, she reminded herself firmly—could turn her on like that!

It was just chemistry, she supposed…but, wow, had it been powerful! She remembered how he had carried her back to bed, making love to her with a control that had driven her crazy with need until she had begged for release, and when that release had come it had been tumultuous. She bit down on her lip as she remembered that complete loss of restraint. It was daunting to think that an enemy could have that amount of power over her. And he'd obviously fully expected to have sex with her; a foil packet had mysteriously appeared when he'd got her into bed.

When she had looked up at him with questioning eyes he had smiled wryly.

'I like to play,' he had murmured. 'But I always play safe.'

Her eyes moved over him contemplatively now. Even in sleep he looked powerfully confident. There was no hint of vulnerability about him. His features were strong, his lips sensually curved. She noticed how long and dark his eyelashes were against his tanned skin, the dark shadow along his square jaw line. Her gaze moved lower to where the white sheet had slipped down to his waist. His torso was wide and muscular, his stomach completely flat. She was suddenly filled with an overwhelming impulse to reach out and touch him, wake him with a kiss, ask him to make love to her again.

Libby curled her hands into tight fists and willed herself not to do any such thing. She had given in to him enough! Last night was a one off.

It took a tremendous effort of will to make herself turn away from him and swing her legs out of the bed, but she did it.

'Where are you going?'

Marc's deep voice made her senses race in chaotic dis-
array, as did the touch of his hand as he trailed it very
softly down the length of her back.

'I'm getting up.' She didn't look around, but instead
reached for her silk dressing gown that was lying on the
floor.

'It's early yet.'

'Yes, but I thought I'd go out, do a little sightseeing
and some shopping.' She forced herself to think
ahead…think of anything except the tantalising prospect
of lying back beside him. Wrapping her dressing gown
around her naked body, she stood up. 'And I suppose you
have important things to do today as well,' she continued
crisply.

'Not really…but I can think of a few things I'd like to
do.' He used the same playful tone that had stirred her
senses so dramatically last night.

Libby flicked a tentative look around at him. He was
sitting propped up against the white pillows now and he
looked so handsome that her heart seemed to turn over.
Did he mean that he wanted her to come back to bed?
The temptation was intense. She imagined herself falling
back into his arms and allowing him to slip her dressing
gown off to pepper sweet kisses all over her body.

Firmly she shut out the thought and tightened the belt
of her gown. 'I hope you realise that last night was just
a bit of fun, Marc,' she said firmly, but even as she spoke
she knew she was trying to convince herself more than
him. 'It didn't mean anything…and it certainly doesn't
mean you can sidetrack me away from the real reason I'm
here.'

'Of course not.' Although his eyes were serious, his

lips twisted in a mocking smile. 'I know you better than to try something like that, Libby.'

'Good.' She swallowed hard on a sudden raw feeling inside. Yes, he did know her…he knew every inch of her body intimately and she had given herself to him more completely than she had done to any other man. Yet aside from that he didn't really know her at all. He thought she was a gold-digger…a charlatan. And he was playing games with her. She wasn't stupid. A man like Marc Clayton would never really be interested in her. She had seen the type of women he went for pictured with him in glossy magazines. He was a multimillionaire tycoon with an opinion of himself; he went for similarly glamorous film stars.

'Well, I'm going to have a shower and then I'm going to go out.' She forced herself to smile brightly at him. 'And I would appreciate it if you would arrange that meeting for me with my father.'

'I'll do that as soon as he arrives, but, as I told you yesterday, he won't be here for a few days.'

'You could ring him now,' she said.

'I could, but I'm not going to.'

The blunt sentence made Libby frown. 'Why not?'

'Because of the time difference, for one thing, and for another your father has a few other meetings and interviews to organise first.'

His cool, businesslike tone infuriated her. 'Well, my time is valuable as well, Marc,' she reminded him. 'Don't forget I've only got four days left before my flight back to London.'

'I haven't forgotten,' he said softly. And before she realised his intentions he had leaned forward, caught hold of her arm and pulled her back down onto the bed.

She lay breathlessly, looking up at him as he rolled over and pinned her firmly beneath him.

'There, that's better.' He smiled down at her with a gleam of satisfaction in his dark eyes. 'After all, if we only have limited time we may as well make the most of it.'

'Marc, I—'

'So where were we?' He cut across her protestations firmly. 'Ah, yes…' His eyes raked over her, taking in the tumble of her dark hair against the white sheets, the fragile beauty of her features. Then his hand moved to untie the belt of her dressing gown. 'Just about here, I think…'

The seductive tone of his voice was followed by an equally seductive kiss. She felt herself melting into him, felt all the reasons for not being in his arms dissolve like snow in spring. All she could say in a rather gruff tone was, 'This probably isn't a good idea…'

He smiled at that. 'I think it is a very…very good idea.'

Then words were lost amidst a much fiercer storm of passion.

When Libby awoke she stretched out a hand to the space next to her in the bed, but it was empty. Pushing her hair out of her eyes, she sat up. She was alone in the bedroom. Marc's clothes were gone from the floor, and except for the dull ache of lethargy in her body it was as if last night…and this morning…had just been a dream.

But it wasn't a dream. She had given herself once again very completely to Marc Clayton.

There was a knock at the door and she felt a sharp dart of anticipation as she hurriedly pulled the sheets more firmly over her naked body, and called for whoever it was to come in.

It was Marion bringing a tray of tea for her, and Libby

didn't know whether to be disappointed that it wasn't
Marc...or relieved.

'*Bonjour, mademoiselle.*' The housekeeper smiled at
her as she put the china tea service down on the dressing
table.

'*Bonjour,* Marion. *Merci,* that is very kind of you,' she
said politely.

Marion reached to straighten the curtains. 'M. Clayton
said you would probably prefer tea to coffee. I hope that
is right?'

'That's fine.' Libby nodded.

The woman smiled. 'Oh, and he says he will pick you
up to take you for lunch in Nice at eleven o clock,'
Marion added casually. 'He said not to be late because he
is on a tight schedule and needs to return home by four.'

'I see.' Libby raked her hand through the darkness of
her hair. Just who the hell did Marc Clayton think he was?
Making love to her as if...as if he owned her! Then issuing orders to her via his housekeeper! She had already
turned down that invitation to lunch yesterday.

She had a good mind to tell Marion to pass a message
back that she would not be free for lunch. There was no
way she wanted him to think she was a complete walk-
over.

However, the prospect of spending time in Nice was
tempting. And maybe turning Marc down again wouldn't
achieve much. What was that old adage about keeping
enemies close? Her heart skipped a couple of apprehensive beats... She certainly couldn't have got any closer
last night!

She lay back against the pillows as Marion left the
room. There was a part of her that still couldn't believe
that she had slept with Marc. She had always been so
very cautious and careful about her relationships. In a way

she was a bit old-fashioned and believed in love and romance going hand in hand…

Taking a deep breath, she pushed the covers back and got up. People had casual flings all the time these days. Marc wouldn't be giving it a second thought and neither should she.

Putting on her dressing gown, she sat down at the table and poured her tea. Outside the window the sky was a perfect blue and already it looked very hot out there. What time was it? she wondered and glanced at her watch. Libby was horrified to see that it was almost ten-thirty; she hadn't slept this late in years! Plus she only had half an hour to shower and get ready!

She was about to rush about frantically and then thought better of it. Marc could wait. It would do him good.

It was eleven-fifteen before Libby was dressed and ready and Marc still hadn't arrived. Not wanting to go downstairs to wait for him, she spent some extra time on her hair and make-up.

She would act cool and sophisticated today, she told herself firmly. There was no way she would let him think that last night was causing her a moment's thought. Despite the pep talk, Libby's emotions were anything but cool as she heard his car pulling up outside.

She flicked a last critical look at her reflection, checking for faults. Her hair was loose around her face to cover the bruise on her forehead, and she wore a smart white knee length skirt and a matching short-sleeved jacket. With it she had teamed a pale pink halter-neck top with matching pale pink very high-heeled shoes. The outfit suited her; she looked stylish, yet young and vibrant.

As she left the bedroom the grandfather clock on the

landing was chiming the half-hour, and she could hear Marc asking Marion where she was.

'I'm up here.' She paused at the top of the stairs and looked down at him in the hall beneath. 'And you are late.'

'Well, I thought if I told you eleven, you would certainly be on time for half past.'

'You are too sure of yourself by far,' she told him lightly, and was very pleased at how blasé and in control she sounded.

Marc watched as she walked down the stairs. She looked wonderful. Her long legs had already acquired a honey-burnished tone from yesterday in the garden, and her dark hair swung glossily around her shoulders.

'You look great.'

The admiration in his tone made her heart flutter a little.

He didn't look bad himself! He was wearing designer blue jeans and a white T-shirt and the casual attire made him look very sexy. As she reached the bottom of the stairs she wanted to lean across and kiss him good morning. Kiss him and kiss him...and never stop.

Her heart was racing now. She moistened her lips, tossed back her long dark hair and stayed well back from him. 'Thanks.' She smiled coolly. 'Actually I wasn't going to join you for lunch, but I changed my mind.'

'Well, I'm glad you did,' he said with a kind of lazy humour that made her senses reel even more. He stepped back to the door and opened it. 'Shall we?' he asked, waiting for her to proceed him out of the door.

She smiled and swept past him, aware that he was watching her every move. It was only as she reached his low-slung sports car that she wondered if perhaps she had worn the wrong outfit; this skirt was a little on the tight side for low vehicles.

Marc opened the car door and waited.

She met his eyes briefly and then hurriedly looked away.

He watched as she sat down and swivelled her legs sideways into the car. It was a difficult manoeuvre, but she managed it.

It was only as she became aware of his eyes moving along the shapely length of her legs that she realised her skirt had ridden up.

Swiftly she pulled it down.

He smiled and slammed the door shut. Libby watched as he walked around and got in beside her. To her consternation he didn't start the engine straight away, but instead turned to look over at her.

'So how are you feeling this morning?' he asked casually.

'Fine.' She felt her skin flare with embarrassed colour. She hoped he wasn't going to talk about what had transpired between them last night!

'No headaches or dizzy spells?' His dark eyes seemed to gleam with a hint of teasing amusement.

'Oh!' Now she could feel herself getting even more hot and bothered. She hadn't realised he was talking about her head. 'No, nothing like that.'

'Good...' He reached out and stroked her dark hair back from her forehead, his eyes on the dull red mark where she had struck it on the concrete.

To her horror, his touch instantly reawakened the desire she felt for him. And she was suddenly very aware of how close he was to her in the confines of the car. The scent of his cologne was tantalisingly familiar from last night; if she leaned her head a little closer she would be in his arms. Her eyes rested on his lips, and red-hot scenes from last night flashed through her mind. Marc making her beg for more...Marc kissing her all over...Marc soothing her and then taking her with a dominance that had taken her breath away.

Libby could hear the steady beat of her heart pounding in her ears.

'Shouldn't we be making a move?' she asked in a husky, tentative whisper.

'What kind of a move were you thinking about?' he asked, his eyes on her lips.

'Very funny, Marc.' With difficulty she looked away from him.

He smiled and to her relief switched on the car engine. 'Sorry. You need to relax, Libby—you look a bit tense. I can assure you I'm not going to pounce on you.'

'And I can assure you I'm not tense,' she snapped, and then, because she did sound a bit tense, added more casually, 'And I didn't think for one moment you were going to pounce on me.' She tried to close out of her mind the way he had pulled her back to bed this morning. 'You're a man of the world, I'm a woman of the world, neither of us have any illusions or hang-ups about...last night.' There she had forced herself to mention it.

'Very grown up.' Marc nodded.

'Exactly.' She smiled at him. 'I'm sure you have a string of very glamorous girlfriends to think about and I have Simon.'

One dark eyebrow lifted at that. 'I don't have a string of girlfriends,' he corrected her. 'I always concentrate on women one at a time.'

'Oh!' What woman was he concentrating on at the moment? she wondered.

He glanced over at her and added sardonically, 'And, correct me if I'm wrong, but you didn't appear to be thinking very hard about Simon last night either.'

Before she could answer that Marc put the car into gear and the car sped down the driveway.

Damn man! she thought in annoyance. He really needed to be taken down a couple of pegs. But all the same she wished she had never mentioned Simon.

He stopped the car to wait for the electric gates to open and glanced over at her. 'Did I upset you by mentioning…your ex, like that?'

Libby wondered if she should stick to her story and tell him that Simon wasn't her ex. But under the circumstances the pretence felt wrong. So she just shook her head.

'I have to tell you, Libby, that last night was very special.'

Of course, he probably said things like that to every woman he slept with, but even so the husky words made her blush with pleasure. Marc watched her closely and there was a dark gleam in his eye as if her reaction satisfied him. Then he reached out and stroked a hand down over the silky softness of her hair. 'So what do you say? Shall we call a truce from any hostilities and just relax and enjoy ourselves today?'

When he touched her like that, looked at her like that, she would have done anything for him, she thought hazily.

'What hostilities?' she asked softly.

He smiled. The gates opened and the car roared through.

Life suddenly felt extraordinarily good as they drove along the coast road towards Nice. Libby leaned back in her seat and watched as Marc handled the powerful sports car with almost as much skill and confidence as he had handled her last night.

As his hand pushed the gear up and then down she

remembered how he had taken her up and down a gear with equal ease and her insides turned to liquid heat.

Trying to take her mind away from sex, she looked at his handsome profile instead. He really was too good looking! It was no wonder all the women seemed to swoon over him.

'Everything OK?' Marc glanced sideways at her and caught her watching him.

'Fine.' She smiled and tried to cover herself by saying, 'I was a million miles away, just thinking about what shopping I'd like to do today.'

'And whether or not your credit card will stand the strain?' He took his eyes off the road to look at her again, raising his eyebrow.

'No!' She frowned and wished for the millionth time she hadn't admitted her credit card debt. 'That's just a temporary glitch, it will be sorted out very soon.'

'I see.' Marc shrugged.

At least, she hoped it would be sorted out very soon, she thought dismally. Simon surely wouldn't expect her to fund him in his new home! He'd pay her back... wouldn't he?

Hell, but she really could pick men! Maybe it was a family curse? Her father didn't seem to have had much luck in his relationships either, and neither had her mother, for that matter!

She raked a hand through her hair and for a moment a ray of pleasure went out of the day.

All she had ever wanted was a settled family life. Very old-fashioned, but there it was. And somehow it just seemed to keep eluding her.

Hastily she turned her mind away from Simon. She could do without him and it was better to be on her own than with the wrong person.

When she got home she was going to find herself a new flat and be completely self-sufficient. Maybe get a cat.

She smiled to herself at the thought.

'What is so amusing?' Marc asked her suddenly.

'Nothing.' She shrugged. 'I was just thinking that maybe I don't need new clothes today. After all, I will be returning home in a few days.'

'Well, it's always good to travel light,' Marc said non-chalantly.

'Yes I suppose, it is.' She shrugged. And in more ways than one, she thought suddenly. Emotional baggage could be just as heavy...if not heavier.

Once she saw her dad she was going to close the chapter on the past and start afresh. She was stronger than she thought...hell, she could even have one-night stands with dangerous, exciting strangers without batting an eyelid.

She looked over at Marc and met his gaze...Well, maybe she wasn't quite as relaxed as she had hoped, she thought hastily as she looked away again. But she was definitely more modern in her outlook than she had been, say, a day ago.

When they reached Nice, Marc parked the car and they strolled along the Promenade des Anglais. The sun was beating down from a clear blue sky and a warm breeze ruffled the sea, sending white-capped waves racing across the bay. They stood for a while admiring the view along the promenade before cutting away from the seafront with its palm trees and chic hotels to wander along a pedestrian zone with stylish boutiques and pavement cafés.

There were some beautiful designer shops and one in particular caught Libby's eye, making her pause outside the window for an extra few minutes.

'That dress would really suit you,' Marc said, nodding towards a very glamorous evening gown.

She shook her head. 'It's absolutely beautiful, but I don't think it would look right on me.'

'Well, I disagree. Come on, let's go in and take a closer look.'

Before Libby could protest Marc was taking her hand and leading her through the door.

It really was an Aladdin's cave inside. Libby had never seen so many exquisite dresses and trouser suits.

Egged on by Marc, she took a few things into the fitting rooms, including the white evening gown.

'Would you like any help, *madame?*' The sales assistant hovered outside the door.

'No, I can manage, thank you.' Libby had just found the price tag on the dress and was recovering from the shock. There was really no point in trying it on because she couldn't afford it. However, as she was already undressed now, she put it over her head.

It looked spectacular. Libby was so amazed that she could only stare at her reflection in wonder. It had shoe-string straps that glittered with heart-shaped rhinestones. But it was the cut of the dress that was especially wonderful; it fell over her curves in a sexy yet subtly flattering way, emphasising her lovely shape, a long split showing her legs as she walked. She looked as if she had the most fantastic figure.

The sales assistant glanced around the door and then smiled at her. 'It is perfect. You must show your husband.'

'Oh he isn't...' But the woman was already opening the doors so that Marc could see her.

'Wow...' Marc gave a long, low whistle. 'You look fabulous.'

Libby had to admit that she did feel good in the dress. She had never possessed anything as beautiful as this.

'You should have it,' Marc said decisively.

Remembering the price tag, Libby shook her head regretfully. 'I don't think so, Marc. The fact is I never go anywhere formal enough to wear something like this.' She tried to be practical.

'But you never know when a dress like that might come in handy.'

Much to the sales assistant's look of disappointment, Libby shook her head. 'No, it is not for me,' she said firmly, before turning back to the fitting room.

As soon as Libby took the dress off, the assistant walked in, picked it up and swept out of the room again.

A few minutes later, when Libby went back out into the shop, Marc was nowhere to be seen and the sales assistant was dealing with another customer. She waved cheerily at Libby when she saw her.

'Thank you, *madame, au revoir.*'

'*Au revoir,*' Libby called back. Stepping out into the street, Libby looked up and down for Marc, but there was no sign of him. She was just about to walk a little further down to look for him when he appeared around the corner.

'Sorry about that,' he said. 'I had to nip back to the car; forgot my mobile phone.'

'That's OK.' Libby smiled.

'That dress looked fabulous on you,' he said as they walked on.

'It was exquisite.' She sighed. 'But did you see the price tag?'

Marc shrugged. 'Ah, but you are worth it!'

Libby grinned. 'I shouldn't have let you persuade me to try it on. It got the sales assistant far too excited.'

'It got me pretty excited as well,' Marc said with a smile.

She glanced up at him. It was strange shopping and laughing like this with him. He was really good fun. Simon would never had been interested in what clothes suited her...and he would never have teased her and flirted so outrageously with her...

She frowned. Marc couldn't be trusted, she reminded herself sternly. He was only being nice to her because he was at a loose end and it served his purposes to keep her away from the press.

'Before we have lunch, perhaps you'd help me buy a few things for Alice.' Marc linked his arm through hers. 'She could do with a few new dresses.'

'That sounds fun,' Libby said, and she meant it. There was something very pleasant about wandering through these bustling streets with him. As they paused outside different shops she admired the architecture of the city, the old bourgeois buildings, their balconies filled with flowers, and the wonderful pale pink and raspberry colours they were painted in.

They passed by the Galleries Lafayette and glanced down the Avenue Jean Medecin where there were lots of other large department stores. It was there that they found a lovely children's boutique.

Libby helped Marc choose several outfits for his daughter. And then insisted he added a cute little teddy bear to his purchases. 'She'll love him,' she said firmly.

'Thanks, Libby.' He smiled at her.

When they stepped back out into the heat of the afternoon a pavement musician had struck up a French tune on the accordion. The music was wonderfully atmospheric and relaxing. People were sitting at cafés under the shade of awnings, tucking into delicious-looking seafood dishes and salad dishes with large glasses of wine.

'I bet you are starving now,' Marc said as he picked up their pace. 'Sorry about that. I should have left the shopping for Alice until later.'

'That's OK. I enjoyed it,' she said honestly.

'Well, you were a big help. Usually I'm at a loss in those places and really miss a woman's eye on the subject.'

'I can't believe that you would ever miss a woman's eye,' Libby said.

'Are you flirting with me, Ms Sheridan?' he asked softly.

'No!' She looked up at him in consternation and he laughed.

'I was kind of hoping you were.' He put his arm around her.

It felt good and she allowed herself to lean against him a little and give into the romantic feeling of the day.

They were down in the old quarter of the city now. It was a picturesque place with a maze of narrow winding streets that had a very Italian feel to them; it reminded Libby that the Italian border wasn't too far away.

'But of course the old part of Nice had quite an Italian influence in bygone days,' Marc said when she remarked on this to him. 'You can still see the Italian names for the streets up alongside the French ones.'

Looking up, Libby could see that the streets did indeed have two names written one on top of the other.

'It makes for a very interesting and rich blend of culture, not to mention the fact that the pasta here is to die for,' Marc continued with a swift smile.

They walked across a wide square and turned a corner into a delightful old flower market. The colourful stalls ran most of the way down the centre of a long plaza and surrounding it were restaurants, their tables and chairs spilling out beneath wide awnings.

It was to one of these restaurants that Marc led her. They sat outside in the shade and Libby watched the world go by and the flower sellers prepare their bouquets.

'It really is lovely here.'

'Yes, very picturesque.' Marc smiled. 'What would you like to drink, Libby?' he asked as he caught the waiter's attention.

'I'd love a glass of white wine, please.'

Marc ordered for her, and then turned his attention back to her across the table.

She was suddenly aware that he seemed to be watching her very closely; his velvet dark eyes warm with an interest that made her stomach flip with a strange kind of exhilaration.

'I'm glad you came out with me today,' he said softly. 'I've really enjoyed your company.'

She felt suddenly shy...crazy when she considered how intimate they had been with each other last night. 'I've enjoyed myself as well,' she said, and then, in case he got the wrong idea, added hastily, 'I mean I wouldn't have wanted to miss seeing Nice. It really is a beautiful city.'

'Of course.' He smiled at her.

For a moment silence fell between them.

It felt like a strangely intimate silence somehow. She wondered what he was thinking as he studied her with those watchful eyes. Was he thinking about last night? The idea made her feel even more self-conscious.

She sought around for something to say to break the feeling. 'When will your ex-wife and your daughter be arriving in town?'

'This evening.'

'Oh, well, that's good. Not long to wait now. I hope Alice likes her new clothes.'

Marc smiled. 'I'm sure she will.'

The waiter arrived with their drinks and as Libby took a sip of her wine she noticed a woman staring at them from a table a little further away. She was young with blonde hair and was very attractive. She also seemed familiar somehow and Libby frowned as she tried to place her.

'Everything OK?' Marc asked her.

'Well…' she lowered her voice '…don't look now, Marc, but there is a woman at a table over there who has been staring at us. And I feel I've seen her somewhere before…but I just can't place her.'

Marc glanced over and his eyes connected with the woman's. 'She's a journalist.'

'Really?' Libby was stunned. 'How do you know?'

'She's interviewed some of my clients.'

'Oh, now I remember where I've seen her before!' Libby smiled at him triumphantly. 'She was at the restaurant you took me to on the night I arrived…do you remember?'

'I remember taking you to the restaurant, but I don't remember seeing her there.'

'Well, she was. She even spoke to me in the restroom…asked me if I was with Marc Clayton! I bet she's the one who rang and arranged for those photographic journalists to come!'

'Really?' Marc's tone was dry.

'Yes, really!' Libby frowned and her heart missed a painful beat. 'You do believe me, don't you?'

'Yes, of course,' he answered her smoothly. Maybe too smoothly, and suddenly Libby wondered if he was just pacifying her by saying that. If really deep down he didn't believe her at all. The thought brought with it all the unpleasant memories from that evening, the way Marc had accused her of being no better than an opportunist...how he had tossed a comment to the reporters about her being just a nobody.

She tried to dismiss the thoughts, tried to tell herself that she and Marc had reached an understanding now. They were enjoying each other's company, for heaven's sake! And he had promised to arrange the meeting with her dad for her.

'Excuse me.' Marc stood up from the table. 'I'll just get rid of her.'

Libby watched as he walked across towards the table and nonchalantly leaned over to talk to the woman.

Although Libby strained her ears, she couldn't make out what they were saying. Not only were they speaking in undertones, but in French. A few moments later the woman got up and left.

'There, all sorted out.' Marc returned to his seat at the table.

'What did you say to her?'

'I told her that her presence here wasn't welcome,' Marc said firmly.

'And what else?'

Marc looked across at her with a raised eyebrow.

'You were talking to her for at least five minutes, Marc.'

'Was I?' Marc shrugged. 'I didn't realise I was being monitored.'

Libby ignored the dry tone. 'Did you ask if it was her at that restaurant that night?'

'No, Libby, I did not.' He shook his head. 'For the simple reason that I believed you when you said it was her.'

'Oh!' She bit down on her lip as a wave of relief surged through her. 'Well, that's OK, then.'

Marc smiled. 'If you really want to know she was asking me the usual questions about my romantic life…was I having an affair with you…' He glanced across at her pointedly and she felt herself blush. 'Or was I going to get back together with my ex-wife.'

Libby looked over at him in surprise and felt her heart do an even deeper dip. 'Is that on the cards?' she asked trying to sound nonchalantly indifferent.

'There has been a rumour circulating for a while.'

'Has there? I haven't heard it!' Libby was stunned.

If Marc wanted to get back with his ex-wife, that was his business, she told herself firmly. Nothing to do with her. What they had shared last night was just a casual fling…no strings…no commitments…no prospect of it being anything else.

Which was fine, she told herself fiercely. So why did she feel so upset?

CHAPTER TEN

THE waiter arrived at the table to take their order and Libby hastily picked up the menu and tried to study it.

Of course she wasn't really upset, she told herself heatedly. She was getting her emotions confused that was all...Maybe because of the passion they had shared last night...Yes, that could be it. Libby latched onto the thought like a lifeline.

'I'll have the Salad Nicoise, please,' she said as she put the menu down again.

She watched as Marc ordered some pasta and then they were left alone again.

'So what did you say to get rid of that journalist?'she asked, trying to switch her thoughts away from her emotions.

'I promised her an exclusive inside story, but only if she vanished straight away.' He smirked.

'The inside story on your reunion with your ex?'

'I didn't specify,' Marc said easily. 'It's best that way, keeps them dangling and hungry for more.'

'Yes, I suppose so.' She shrugged.

Libby toyed with her glass, and tried to stop herself asking any questions about him getting back with his ex. She lasted about five minutes. 'So is there any truth in these rumours?'

'Is there any truth in the rumour that you are getting back together with Simon?' he prevaricated.

Libby shrugged and didn't know what to say to that. If she said no her smokescreen would be gone...and she had her pride. 'I don't know what will happen between Simon and I.'

'Why did you split up in the first place?'

The personal question made her very uncomfortable, but she answered him truthfully. 'I suppose it was because I wanted children and he didn't,' she said huskily. 'I mean, he didn't say that or anything...but...' She shrugged. 'If I'm honest that problem was always there between us in the background.'

'That's a big problem to overcome,' Marc said softly.

'Yes...' She took a sip of her wine.

'If you want my opinion, the man is a fool.'

The gentle words made her go warm inside. She tried to ignore the glow...tried to think sensibly. 'Thanks for the vote of confidence.' She looked over at him. 'But aren't you the man who thinks I'm a gold-digger?'

The question lay between them and when Marc didn't immediately answer her the silence turned incredibly painful. Libby took another sip of her wine and tried to tell herself she didn't care what he thought of her. 'See, I rest my case.' She managed to say the words flippantly as if she didn't care.

'Libby, I—' Whatever Marc was about to say was cut off by the ring of his mobile phone. 'Excuse me.' He took the phone out of his pocket, answered it impatiently, and then switched to speaking in French.

Their food arrived just as his conversation came to a close. 'Sorry about that, Libby,' Marc said as he snapped the phone closed. 'It was Pierre, my assistant; he's picking up one of my clients from the airport today.'

'Which client is that?' Libby asked idly.

Marc hesitated. 'Rebecca Bouchet.'

'Another A-list celebrity,' Libby murmured. 'You certainly mingle with the best.'

'But of course.' He raised his eyebrows. 'How is your salad?'

'It's very tasty.' Libby toyed with the food; it was lovely, but in truth she seemed to have lost her appetite.

'So, Libby.' Marc reached for his glass. 'Tell me, why is it so important to you now that you see your father again?'

The sudden question took her by surprise. 'I thought you already knew the answer to that,' she answered glibly. 'For his money, of course.'

One dark eyebrow rose. 'I was being serious.'

'So was I.' She held his gaze across the table.

Marc noted the shadows in her blue eyes, the vulnerable twist of her lips.

'You see, I really can't comprehend why you need to ask me that question,' she said softly. 'The simple fact is that it's twenty years since my dad walked out. I don't know why and I don't know where he went. Wouldn't you wonder about your dad? Wouldn't you want to fill in the intervening blank years and see him?'

'Well, my relationship with my dad is possibly a lot different to yours.'

'Yes, it most probably is,' Libby said quickly. 'But I thought I had a good relationship with my dad…maybe mistakenly, but there you go…' She shrugged. 'And the fact remains that after all these years I've still got questions to ask. Obviously I know the reason my parents' marriage broke down was because my mum fell in love with someone else, but I don't know why. I don't have any details about why she fell out of love with my dad…'She trailed off. She had been going to say she didn't know why her mum had told her her dad was dead, but such a revelation was too personal…and out of loyalty to her mum, not one to be aired.

'You don't know why?' Marc prompted her gently.

Libby shook her head. 'I don't know why my relationship with my dad had to break down as well,' she finished
instead, her voice husky. 'I could never have a discussion
with my mother on the subject. That was always taboo.
So I suppose I just want to put the past to rest now…learn
by its mistakes…which probably sounds stupid but…' she
shrugged '…there it is.'

There was silence for a moment. 'No, that doesn't
sound stupid,' Marc said gently.

Libby met his gaze across the table. 'I don't expect
anything from him apart from his time. Half an hour and
I'll walk away.'

Marc nodded. 'I will tell him, Libby. He's due to phone
tonight.'

Libby looked over at him with a frown. 'You could
give him my phone number if you'd like?'

'I don't think that would help, really.'

'Why not?'

'Because he's…out of the country and I think he feels
a bit apprehensive about talking to you. He'd rather meet
face to face.'

Libby nodded. 'Well, I have to admit it would be easier
than talking on the phone.'

'So we will leave it like that,' Marc said firmly.

'Yes.' Libby wanted to ask him if he believed now that
she wasn't a gold-digger, but she feared she might not
like the answer and the question stuck in her throat.
Maybe he was right and they should just leave the conversation there.

'So what is your relationship like with your dad?' she
asked lightly instead. 'Now that I've bared my soul you
should tell me a little about yourself at least.'

'There is really not much to tell. I've always got on

extremely well with him.' Marc smiled wryly. 'He and my mother were married for forty years and raised three children and, although they had their occasional arguments, they were blissfully happy.'

'That's a big achievement in today's age of divorce,' Libby said wistfully.

'Yes, tell me about it. My divorce came as a big shock. But the family rallied around and they were supportive, which meant a lot in those dark days.'

'Why did you get divorced?'

'Well...our romance was a whirlwind courtship. We met when Marietta came into my office to talk about my representing her. Eight weeks later we were married.'

'That sounds romantic,' Libby said quietly.

'Yes, it was, and it seemed like the right thing to do at the time. Marietta was pregnant, we were both very excited and...' Marc trailed off. 'Well, basically, I don't think either of us had thought it through properly. We tried to make a go of it, but Marietta's job as an actress was such that it took her away a lot. She had an affair with her leading man.'

'Oh, Marc, I'm sorry. That must have been awful for you.'

'It wasn't a pleasant time. I practically had to bribe the press to shut the story down. We tried to pick up the pieces and carry on, but we couldn't put things back together.'

'How long is it since you divorced?'

'Two years now.' His lips twisted wryly. 'There's been a lot of water under the bridge since then.'

'And now you are thinking of giving the relationship another go?' The question felt hollow inside her.

Marc shook his head. 'I don't think so, Libby. For Alice's sake it's enough that we've salvaged a good friendship. We should just have remained friends in the first place. I don't think either of us were thinking straight when we tied the knot.'

'I see.' It was ridiculous to feel happy about the fact that he wasn't getting back with his ex. It was nothing to do with her, she told herself firmly. 'Well, it's good that you're friends.'

'Yes, it is.' Marc nodded. 'Alice's welfare is the most important thing to me.'

The words stirred something inside Libby. 'I think that is really lovely,' she said seriously.

For a moment their eyes held across the table. She really liked Marc, she thought suddenly. And his attitude towards his child seemed in such marked contrast to her father's as she'd grown up. The thought crept in unwelcome and unwanted. That wasn't fair; she didn't know the truth about her dad, she reminded herself firmly. Maybe something had happened to prevent him from coming back…maybe her stepfather had threatened him? Sean had certainly been nasty enough for that, but then again maybe her dad just hadn't really been interested enough to return.

Marc watched the sudden shadows flick through Libby's expression.

Carl was still firmly maintaining that he had tried to get in contact with Libby, but that she hadn't wanted to see him until now. And he was not at all happy about her turning up here; he thought the timing was appalling. The business side of Marc was bound to agree. Yet when Libby talked about the past there was a delicate vulnerability about her that touched him.

Marc frowned and tried to remember his business obligations.

'Would you like another drink?'

Libby shook her head.

'Well, maybe we should go.' Marc glanced at his watch. 'Unfortunately I have an appointment at four.'

The drive back along the coast was made mostly in silence. Libby wished she knew what Marc Clayton was thinking. He looked pensive, she thought, as if his mind was a million miles away.

When he pulled the car to a halt by the front door he turned to look at her and Libby could feel the familiar swirl of chemistry between them, it was a heavy, potent feeling and it clouded and veiled all other thoughts.

'Well, thanks for a lovely afternoon,' she said quietly.

'My pleasure.'

'Do you want to come in, or are you rushing?'

Marc glanced towards the clock on the dashboard. 'I guess I have time to come in and have a coffee.'

As they went into the house Libby wondered if it had been a mistake inviting him in. What about acting cool? she reminded herself. Trouble was, she really didn't want to act cool. And she was glad he had come in.

'Now you'll have to point me in the direction of the kitchen,' she said, trying to cover the sudden feeling of awkwardness.

'Second door on the left.' He smiled at her.

'I won't be stepping on Marion's toes making coffee, will I?' she asked as she made her way down the corridor.

'No, Marion will be over in her own part of the house and won't be back here until it's time to start dinner at seven.' Marc paused by the front door. 'I've forgotten my phone again. Won't be a minute.'

Libby went on into the kitchen. It was a very large and modern room with white cupboards, dark granite work surfaces and stainless-steel accessories. At one side there was a seating area looking out towards the garden.

What she wouldn't give to have a kitchen like this at home, Libby thought as she filled the kettle and found some cups.

She smiled over at Marc as he came in.

'This is such a lovely house.'

'Yes, it's OK.' He leaned back against the worktop and watched as she made the coffee. She looked extremely sexy, he thought idly.

'You sound very blasé,' she said. 'Obviously you are used to perfection.'

'I suppose I am.' He caught hold of her arm as she made to walk past him. 'You were pretty damn perfect in that dress this afternoon.' He murmured the words in an undertone.

Libby looked up at him and felt as if she were drowning in the darkness of his eyes, could feel the twist of sexual attraction stronger than ever between them.

Marc reached out and touched the side of her face lightly. 'Shall we forget about the coffee?' he asked huskily.

How was it that just the slightest brush of his fingertips against her skin set her alight? she wondered hazily.

'I thought you were in a hurry for an appointment?' She tried desperately to hold back from him.

'I can reschedule,' he murmured, brushing a fingertip lightly over her lips in a teasing, provocative caress. Then his mouth covered hers; there was naked hunger in the kiss and it made her body throb with excitement.

She felt his hands move up under her top, pushing her flimsy bra away, exposing the smooth curves of her body to the demands of his touch.

For a moment Libby gave herself up to the wild and wonderful torment of his kisses, then as she felt his hands starting to pull up her skirt she drew away.

'Not here…Marc.'

'Why not?' As he spoke he picked her up and sat her on the counter-top. He kissed her again, and the passion was so intense it drugged her senses. She kissed him back heatedly.

Her jacket was discarded, her top followed and a few moments later she was only wearing her skirt.

Libby had given up even trying to desist. She felt powerless in the grip of her desires; all she could think about was how much she wanted him.

'Hold on.' Marc was the one to pull back. 'We'll have to adjourn and go upstairs; I left the protection there.'

This was probably Libby's chance to gather her senses and pull back from the situation. But she didn't want to pull back. So she allowed him to take her hand and lead her out of the room and up the stairs.

When Libby opened her eyes she could hear the sound of the shower in the *en suite* bathroom. The room was in darkness and she felt disoriented, not knowing what time of the day or night it was. Shakily she reached out a hand and switched on the bedside lamp.

It was seven in the evening! Marc had missed his appointment. She smiled to herself as she remembered the heat of their passion. It had been wild and exhausting, but it had also been totally and utterly wonderful. She had thought their lovemaking last night and this morning was good…but this had been even more incredible. Her mind drifted lazily back over the events… How was it that Marc was able to turn her on like that? Why did her body respond so ardently to him, and her senses soar?

She even loved the sound of his voice, the gentle, seductive way he cradled her in his arms afterwards and murmured sweet nothings into her ear.

I'm in love with him…The thought hit her out of nowhere. I'd do anything for him.

Wildly she tried to backtrack. But the plain facts were inescapable. No other man had ever made her feel the way Marc did. She had given herself to him so completely because her emotions were completely overwhelmed by her feelings for him. She had tried to hide from them… put her behaviour down to chemistry…pure sex…told herself she didn't even like him! But the truth was she was head over heels in love. That was the reason she had been so upset when she had thought Marc was going to get back with his ex-wife. And the reason why it hurt so badly that he thought she was a gold-digger.

Did he still think that?

Libby really didn't know the answer to that, but, remembering how tenderly he had just held her, it was hard to imagine that he did. And suddenly she dared to hope that this might not just be a few snatched hours of bliss, but the start of something wonderful.

Libby pushed the bedclothes down and got up out of the bed. She shouldn't be thinking like this. The situation was too precarious to hope.

She glanced around for her clothes, and then remembered how she had very nearly made love with Marc in the kitchen! Her bra and her jacket were probably still lying down there on the floor. And Marion would be going in there to make dinner!

A wave of embarrassment washed through her and hurriedly she pulled on a pair of black trousers and a white T-shirt that were sitting on the bedroom chair. 'Marc, I won't be a moment, I'm just going downstairs,' she called out. But he obviously couldn't hear her over the noise of the shower.

Libby practically ran downstairs and into the kitchen. To her relief there was no sign of Marion yet. She retrieved her jacket from the counter-top and then had to bend down and pick up her bra from beneath one of the comfortable seats under the window. As she straightened she saw a newspaper pushed under the cushion of the chair, and something made her pull it out to take a closer look.

The paper was a local one, but it was in English and the first thing she saw was a picture of her father.

CARL QUINTON ARRIVES IN CANNES FOR THE FILM FESTIVAL.

The words jumped out at Libby, and a very cold feeling gripped her as she glanced at the date. It was yesterday's paper!

Marc had told her categorically that her father wasn't arriving for a few days!

With a sick feeling she ran her eyes over the rest of the article.

Carl Quinton, thirty-nine...

Thirty-nine! Well that was definitely wrong, Libby thought wryly. With difficulty she read on.

...has had an exciting few years. Following his success in the Broadway show *ABE* his rise to fame has been meteoric. Now it seems that his romantic life is also set to soar, for it is rumoured that he and his co-star Julia Hynes have fallen in love. Ms Hynes, who is twelve years his junior, is said to be shopping for a wedding trousseau in Paris before flying down to Cannes to join him for the première of their film.

How much of that was true? Libby wondered. They had certainly got her father's age wrong. He was forty-five.

Her eyes moved to the last paragraph.

Carl Quinton has been married three times and has a daughter from his first marriage. Sadly Carl's daughter has shunned him over the years despite his numerous attempts to see her.

Had Marc Clayton fed the columnist that scurrilous piece of information? It certainly sounded like it. Libby felt her heart starting to hit against her chest with a painful momentum.

And was it true that her father was already here? Half of her wanted to believe that the paper had got that wrong. She didn't really want to consider that Marc had lied to her like that.

But as she looked again at the photograph she noticed that it had been taken in Cannes. Her father was standing on the Croisette; she recognised the Carlton flags waving in the breeze behind him.

So Marc *had* lied to her! The knowledge made the cold feeling inside her intensify. No wonder he had been in such a hurry to move her out of Cannes! He'd deliberately misled her, brought her here to keep her out of the way...

Her heart beat fiercely as she remembered how easily she had allowed him to do all that. OK, she had known that he didn't exactly think her motives for being here were wonderful, but she had thought they had transcended beyond that. She had actually believed him when he had promised to set up a meeting for her with her father.

And had imagined herself in love with him.

Her heart froze as she remembered the foolish thoughts that had flown through her mind just a few moments ago!

And how she had actually dared to hope that Marc might be feeling something for her, when in reality he must be laughing at her! He was toying with her, amusing himself with her, and she had willingly gone along with it. Had given herself to him totally.

Remembering how wild and abandoned her responses had been to him, all she could think about now was what a fool she had been and the cold, numb feeling started to change into furious waves of anger.

For a moment she stood indecisively, and wondered what to do. Should she confront Marc with her knowledge, or play it cagey, see if she could glean anything out of the situation? Hearing footsteps in the hallway, she took the impulsive decision to play dumb and hastily pushed the paper back under the cushion.

Marion came into the room and looked over at her in surprise. '*Bonsoir, madamoiselle!*'

'*Bonsoir.*'

Libby could see the woman's glance moving towards the chair. 'I was just collecting my jacket, I left it in here earlier.' It was an effort to smile. Did Marion know that Marc was keeping her father's presence in Cannes a secret?

'I was just about to start preparing dinner, *mademoiselle*. Will *Monsieur* Clayton be joining you?' the housekeeper asked.

'Not this evening.' Libby hesitated. 'And actually I think I'll skip dinner as well, Marion. Would you be so kind as to call a taxi for me?'

Marion hesitated. 'My husband can drive you wherever you want to go.'

Libby was damn sure she didn't want anyone spying on her, telling Marc where she was going. 'That won't be necessary, Marion. If you'd just call a taxi that would be

great, thank you.' Aware that Marion looked a bit discon-
certed, Libby headed out into the hallway.

Taking control of the situation was making her feel a
bit better. OK, Marc obviously wasn't going to keep his
promise and arrange a meeting for her with her father...but that didn't mean she couldn't take matters into
her own hands. She would find out where her father was
and she would go there herself.

Libby was about to go back into the bedroom when she
heard Marc's voice from within and paused. He was talking to someone on the phone.

She pressed her head a little closer to the door.

'Sorry to miss our meeting,' Marc was saying briskly.
'I had some unfinished business to deal with.'

He was describing her as unfinished business! Libby
felt herself go hot inside with hurt and with shame.

'Yes, well, I'm running late now. I'm due to have dinner with Marietta in half an hour, so can we meet tomorrow instead, say about ten?'

Dinner with Marietta sounded cosy. Was that another
lie? Libby wondered. Was he dating his ex-wife?

'OK, Carl...I'll see you then.'

Carl. He was talking to her father...Libby's hands
curled into fists that were so tight her nails dug deep into
the softness of her flesh.

Did her father even know that she was already in town?
Maybe Marc was playing them off against each other,
telling her he wasn't here and vice versa. The thought
struck her suddenly and it seemed very possible.
Obviously Marc was the one in control. He had replied
to her email, he had picked her up from the airport...He
had moved her out here and made sure she was in Nice
rather than Cannes today so that there was no possibility
of them bumping into each other.

And he was a sharply astute and ruthless businessman who had invested time and money into her father's career, she reminded herself firmly. He didn't want anything to distract from Carl's success.

Snippets of previous conversations flitted through her mind.

'I'm a businessman first and foremost, Libby,' he had warned her bluntly. 'And I suggest you bear that in mind before you play any more games. If there are to be winners and losers in this, then I have no intention of being the loser.'

She had been such an idiot, Libby thought painfully. He had even warned her up front. So how could she have allowed herself to be swept along by his lies and his deceitful games?

Libby could hear him moving around the bedroom. Any minute now he was going to walk out here and catch her loitering outside the door.

Taking a deep breath, she forced herself to go back in and face him.

'I was wondering where you had got to.' Marc looked over at her and smiled. He was fully dressed and had just sat down on the edge of the bed to put his shoes on. His eyes were warm...his manner relaxed.

'I remembered I'd left my clothes in the kitchen.' She tried to smile back at him. 'And I thought I'd better pick them up before Marion is too shocked.'

'Ah, yes. Good thinking. We wouldn't want to shock Marion.' For the first time she noticed the languid amusement in his tone, in his eyes. 'I'd like to have made love to you in the kitchen. Next time I'll remember to come prepared...' His voice was teasing and seductive.

Libby wanted to fiercely tell him there would be no next time. But she forced herself to remain silent.

'Are you OK?'

'Yes, fine.'

Marc stood up from the bed and before she could move out of his reach he pulled her closer and put a hand under her chin, tipping her face up so that she was forced to look at him. 'Are you sure you are OK?' he asked softly.

The concern in his tone and the warmth of his dark eyes made her heart turn over. She suddenly wished everything were OK…and she could just melt in against him again…kiss him again. But that was crazy. Marc was playing with her…using her and she couldn't let it continue.

'Everything is fine,' she said shakily.

'Good.' He smiled and for a moment his eyes lingered on her lips. 'You know, you've made me forget about my appointment and that is something I would never normally do.'

'Work always comes first,' she added dryly. 'Yes, I know that about you.'

Marc stroked a hand lightly down the side of her face and she could feel her temperature rising. 'And I'm afraid I won't be able to get back here this evening. So I'll have to see you in the morning.'

'That's fine. I didn't expect you to come back.' Would he be staying overnight with Marietta? she wondered. Not that she gave a damn, she told herself brusquely! She knew now how irrational she had been imagining herself in love with him. It had been stupid in the extreme.

'You sound tense.' He nibbled on the side of her ear. 'Let me unwind you,' he murmured gruffly.

The feeling of his lips against her skin made little shivers of desire instantly shoot through her. She wanted to turn and kiss him; the need was so great it was like a physical ache inside and at the same time she hated herself for the weakness. Hastily she pulled away.

'Don't, Marc!'

Marc smiled. 'No, you're right, I'd better not otherwise I will never get out of this house tonight.' He glanced at his watch, and then turned to pick up his wallet from next to the bed.

'By the way, I've left you a little something.'

Libby watched as he walked across to the wardrobe and took out a cardboard box with a designer name on it. 'There.' With a look of sly satisfaction he put it down on the bed. 'You can open it when I've gone.'

'What is it?' Libby asked suspiciously.

'I told you, open it when I leave—'

'I'd rather open it now.' Libby reached out and flicked the lid off, then folded back the tissue paper to look at what was inside.

'It's the dress you tried on today,' Marc said when she did nothing but stare at it.

'Yes, I can see that.' Libby fingered the delicate material and fury licked through her body. And suddenly there was no chance that she was going to play this cool. 'Is this my payment?'

'Sorry?' He turned to look at her with a frown. 'I don't follow you?'

'Well, obviously gold-diggers like me want some remuneration.' Her voice trembled with fury. 'So I take it this is mine.'

'I bought you the dress because you looked sensational in it and I thought you would like it,' Marc answered coolly.

Libby put the lid back on the box. 'Well, the thing is, Marc, that I am not quite that cheap. If you want to buy me off it will cost you a lot more than a mere designer dress.'

'What the hell is that supposed to mean?'

'Oh, don't look so surprised, Marc. After all, you know the real truth about me, don't you?' Her voice dripped with sarcasm. 'Our little fling has been all very well, but I think we can drop the pretence now, don't you?'

'What pretence is that?' Marc asked, his eyes narrowed on her intently.

'You know damn well the pretence I'm talking about.' She pushed a hand through her hair impatiently. 'My father is here in Cannes. You've lied to me.'

'Ah, I see.'

The very calmness of his tone infuriated her. 'Is that all you can say? You have led me down the garden path, Marc Clayton. You have lied to me and deceived me...and all you can say is, "Ah, I see."'

'Libby, calm down.' He walked a step closer and she held up a hand.

'Just stay away from me.'

'I promised you a meeting with your father and I intend to deliver on that,' he said smoothly.

'When were you thinking of doing that? The year two thousand and twenty?' Her voice grated unevenly. 'Does my father even know I'm here?'

Marc looked suddenly uncomfortable.

'No, I thought not!' Libby glared at him with bright, furious eyes. 'You bastard, Marc!'

He raked a hand through the darkness of his hair. 'Look, Libby, this is not an easy situation.'

'Well, it's been easy for you. I've made it easy, and you've conned me and walked all over me.'

'I haven't conned you—'

'That is a matter of opinion.' Libby brushed past him

nd opened her wardrobe door and without even pausing
or thought she got her canvas bag out from the top and
tarted to throw her clothes into it. She didn't even bother
o fold anything, it all just got jammed in any old way.

'Libby, what are you doing?'

'I would have thought that was obvious. I'm getting
ut of here.'

'You can't go like this,' he said quietly. 'We need to
it down and talk properly.'

How could he sound so serene when inside she was
urning up with fury?

'I've done all the talking I want to do. And I have
bsolutely nothing more to say to you.' She deliberately
eft the dress Marc had bought for her on the bed and
ipped up her bag. Then she turned to look at him. As
heir eyes met she felt a flicker of pain deep inside for
vhat might have been...for the old feelings he had stirred
n her...the way he could kiss her and melt every sinew
n her body, the way he had made her feel so special when
he lay in his arms...Very quickly she squashed those
motions. It had all been a lie. Everything had been a lie.

'I don't want you to leave, Libby...not like this.'

'Oh, I know you don't.' Her voice dripped with sar-
asm. 'You want me to stay here out of harm's way while
ou control the press. Well, guess what, Marc...I don't
;ive one toss about what you want. I've enjoyed the fling,
ut now I'm doing things my way.' She tossed her dark
air over her shoulder and lifted her bag up.

Marc was standing by the door.

'Please get out of my way,' she told him coldly.

Marc hesitated. 'Libby, I don't know where you think
ou are going. This house is miles from the nearest town,
ou can't walk anywhere.'

'I said get out of my way.' She raised her chin and fixed him with a very determined look.

For a moment she thought he wasn't going to do as she asked. Then with a shrug he stood back.

She swept past him, her head held high.

'So where are you going?' he asked as he followed her out onto the landing.

'None of your business.' She walked down the stairs and called for Marion.

'*Oui, mademoiselle?*' The woman came out of the kitchen.

'Did you manage to phone that taxi for me?' Libby asked breezily.

'*Ah, non…*' Marion flicked an uncertain glance up towards Marc. 'The line was busy, *mademoiselle.*'

'Well, perhaps then your husband will drive me into town?'

Again Marion looked up towards Marc for confirmation.

'Do as Libby asks, please, Marion,' Marc told her calmly.

The housekeeper nodded. 'One moment *mademoiselle,*' she said politely and turned to go down the corridor towards the other side of the house.

'Jacques will drop you anywhere you want to go, Libby,' Marc said quietly.

Libby made no reply. She wasn't going to say thank you.

'Listen, why don't we arrange to have breakfast tomorrow so we can talk things over?' Marc said smoothly.

Libby ignored him and walked out of the front door, closing it quietly behind her.

A few moments later a long black stretched limousine crunched over the gravel drive and pulled up beside her.

CHAPTER ELEVEN

THERE was a storm brewing. Libby could see flashes of lightning playing over the sea from the darkened windows of the limousine; they lit up the night like a searchlight turning the sea and the mountains to silver like a reverse negative on a roll of film.

But Libby's mind wasn't on the storm; it was on the conversation she had just had with Marc. She supposed she should have played it cooler, pretended she didn't know he was lying to her, bided her time. Then perhaps she would have found out exactly where her father was. Instead her defences and her control had cracked, in the same way the forks of lightning were splitting the darkness of the sky now.

One moment she had been determined to keep calm and play him at his own game…and the next her calm resolve had gone, buried under much more complex feelings of hurt.

She really had for a crazy moment imagined that she was in love with him!

A roar of thunder tore through the silence of the night and then the rain started. It drummed wildly against the car window like a continuous sheet of water, the sound echoing her heartbeats, echoing the tears that were welling up inside just thinking about Marc.

With determination she pulled herself together. She wasn't going to allow Marc Clayton to upset her, she told herself firmly. He wasn't worth it!

She opened her handbag and found a comb for her hair

and put on some lipstick. She didn't want to arrive back at her hotel looking a mess.

They were in Cannes now. The lights along the Croisette reflected on the wet road in a mosaic of colour. The sea was a dark swirl lit by the occasional flash of lightning. Libby watched as the hotels and buildings swished by.

She could see the Carlton hotel up ahead. And suddenly she was remembering her father's picture in the paper. The Carlton beach had been behind him, the flags from the hotel had been clearly visible.

'Did you say you wanted the Rosette hotel?' Jacques asked her suddenly from the front.

'Actually, will you drop me outside the Carlton?' Libby asked impulsively.

'*Oui, Mademoiselle.*'

'Would you mind waiting for me?' Libby asked as the car slowed and she looked up towards the impressive entrance. She didn't want to be lugging her old piece of luggage with her in there, she thought wryly.

'Certainly, *Mademoiselle.*'

As Libby reached for the door handle it was opened for her from the outside. She looked out and saw a doorman waiting for her with an umbrella ready to shield her from the rain.

'*Merci.*' She smiled at the man as she headed past him and through the glass doors into an impressive lobby.

The air of elegance about the hotel was striking. For a moment Libby was distracted from her mission as she looked around in appreciation. Then she walked forward to the desk where a receptionist was dealing with an attractive young woman wearing a designer black trouser suit.

As Libby waited she absent-mindedly admired the

woman's Gucci cases and tried not to think about how
nervous she felt about the prospect of finally seeing her
father again.

'Can I help you, *madame?*' Another receptionist
stepped forward.

'Yes, I hope so.' Libby smiled at him. 'I was wondering
if you could tell me if you have a Mr Carl Quinton staying
here?'

The receptionist shook his head apologetically. 'Ah,
madame, I regret I cannot give you this information. I
hope you will understand? It is classified.'

'Yes, of course.' Libby smiled at him. She supposed
she should have known that would be the answer, but
even so Libby couldn't help feeling disappointed. 'I shall
just have to contact him in some other way. Perhaps I
could write a note for him and leave it with you... Just
in case he checks in?'

'You may, and *if* he checks in I will be sure to give it
to him.' The receptionist smiled at her and handed her
across some hotel notepaper.

'Thank you.' As Libby picked up a pen she noticed the
woman who had been in front of her glancing around.
And with a start Libby recognised her as Julia Hynes, the
star of her father's film, and if the papers were to be
believed the woman her father was going to marry!

She was about Libby's age and exceptionally slim and
beautiful with long blonde hair and classically perfect features.

'If you'd like to sign here, please, *mademoiselle?*' The
receptionist spoke to Julia and she turned away. 'And we
will arrange for someone to bring your luggage up to your
room.'

Libby wondered if she should go across to her, tell

her she was Carl's daughter and ask if her father would
see her.

Before she could move the lift doors opened and a few
more people entered the lobby. There was a buzz of excitement as Julia Hynes was recognised and she was lost
from Libby's sight as a crowd started to gather around
her asking for autographs.

Then Libby saw her being greeted by a man in a smart
black suit.

'Darling, it's so good to see you.' The woman's heartfelt tones drifted above other voices.

The man embraced her and as he turned slightly
Libby's breath froze in her throat. It was her father, she
recognised him instantly.

Their eyes met and held across the busy concourse, and
she could see the recognition in his expression, could see
he knew exactly who she was. For a moment it was as if
everyone else melted away. Libby could feel her heart
thudding so heavily against her chest that it hurt.

He really didn't look that different. Yes, he was older;
there were a few silver hairs at his temples, a few lines
at the corners of his blue eyes, but apart from that he
looked the same... Except that he was different. It was
hard to define. It was as if he was the same on the outside,
but that spark of warmth inside...that way he'd had of
smiling at her that had made him special and 'her dad'
had gone...

Julia was saying something about Paris being just di-
vine, before continuing on to say, 'Oh, and a few moments ago a woman was asking about you at the desk. Is
it someone you know? I think she is still here...' Julia
started to turn around.

Carl looked away from Libby and put his arm through

hers. 'Julia, I can't see anyone I know in here. Let's go, darling. I want to hear all about Paris over dinner.'

Shock sizzled through Libby, but somehow she gathered herself together and, leaving the blank piece of paper on the desk, she turned to walk out of the hotel. Obviously her father didn't want to see her, and if that was the case she wasn't going to walk over to him. She had her pride.

It was a relief to climb into the limousine and hide behind the tinted glass away from prying eyes.

All right, she had only been seven when her father had walked out, but she knew he had recognised her; she had seen that look of recollection in his eyes. He'd known she was his daughter...yet he had still turned away.

He hadn't wanted to know her!

'Where to, *Mademoiselle?*'

The driver's voice cut into her thoughts.

She only hesitated for a second before saying huskily. 'Jacques, would you take me to the airport, please?'

'Yes, of course, *Mademoiselle.*'

As the limousine sped through the darkness of the evening Libby wished she could wave a magic wand and just be home in the security of her own flat. And she wished more than anything that she had never come here.

Afterwards that trip to Nice airport just seemed like a blur. She thanked the driver as he dropped her off outside the main terminal building, and she hurried inside.

The airport was busy and she had to wait a while before someone could deal with her at a desk. Her air ticket home was useless as it was for a few days' time, so she had to purchase another one. It seemed to take an age to sort out, as the time and availability of a flight to London was checked.

The only available seat was on a flight at two the next morning. Libby glanced at her watch. It was only nine-thirty now, but although it sounded like an interminable time to wait she slid her credit card across and booked it. All she wanted was to go home.

The check-in desk for her flight didn't open for over an hour, so she was stuck with her luggage until then. Carrying her bag over towards a café, she bought herself a glass of mineral water and waited. For a while she watched lovers embrace, families say goodbye and the flight information boards flick over. All of life seemed to pass her by.

She remembered how hopeful she had been when she arrived here. Hopeful that she would, not only find her father, but return to a time and place in life when she had loved someone deeply and felt loved in return. Remembering the expression in her father's eyes as he'd turned away from her, she realised how foolish that hope had been. You could never go back in time because nothing stayed the same. You could only move forward.

And then there was Marc. She realised now that she had got it wrong when she had accused him of not telling her dad she was here. But that still didn't change the fact that he had lied to her about her father's whereabouts…used her. And he'd probably been the one to tell the press that she had shunned her father for years. Marc would do whatever it took to protect his business interests. Hard to believe when he had kissed her so passionately, made love to her so ardently. But lovemaking for him was probably just a recreational pastime. He was probably with his ex-wife now, having a sophisticated supper… A cold, gnawing ache sprang up inside her.

She really couldn't bear to think about Marc.

'Libby?'

The familiar tone took her very much by surprise and as she looked up into Marc's dark eyes she thought for a moment that she was imagining things. But she wasn't imagining it; he was standing next to her table looking directly at her, and her heart lurched crazily.

'What are you doing here?' she asked huskily.

Marc smiled. 'I've come to find you, of course.'

He was so indolently confident that it brought back her fighting spirit. 'Well, you shouldn't have done,' she said in annoyance.

He pulled out the chair opposite her. 'May I sit down?'

'I'd rather you didn't.'

He ignored that and sat down anyway, and a small part of her...the absolutely mad part that was glad he had ignored her...was glad he was here.

To counteract that silly emotion she glared at him. 'Just go away, Marc.'

'We have things to sort out,' he said calmly.

'I don't think so.' She took a sip of her water and tried to regain control of her emotions. 'Shouldn't you be having dinner with your ex-wife?'

He didn't look surprised that she knew this. 'Yes, but under the circumstances I thought it best to cancel.'

'What's the matter, Marc? Frightened that you have a loose cannon on your hands?' she grated sardonically. 'Scared I might run to the press and malign your client? Is that why you are here?'

'No. And I don't think for one moment that you are going to do that.'

'No?' Libby fixed him with a perceptive stare. 'I take it this is the point in the conversation where you offer me a pay-off?'

'No.' Marc shook his head. 'This is the point in the conversation when I tell you I've come to take you to see your father.'

The remark took Libby by surprise. 'Why now?'

'Because I am a man of my word, Libby. I promised you that I would arrange a meeting for you and I have.'

'Well, it's too late for that now.' As she lifted the glass of water to her lips again she was alarmed to find that her hand was shaking. Hurriedly she put the glass back down again and hoped that Marc hadn't noticed, but she could see his eyes watching her, noting her every movement.

'It's not too late,' he said gently.

'For me it is,' she said firmly. 'Apart from anything else I have booked and paid for a flight to London.'

'Can I see your ticket?'

The calm question puzzled her. 'Why do you want to see my ticket? Don't you believe me? Do you think I'm just sitting here for the good of my health?'

'I believe you, Libby. I just want to see it.'

'Well, if it will make you go away…' She grabbed her handbag, took out the ticket and slid it across to him.

She watched as he opened it. 'Flight at two a.m.,' he murmured. 'I don't think you are going to be able to make that, Libby.'

'I—'

Before she could stop him he had put the ticket away into the inside pocket of his jacket.

'Marc, what the hell do you think you are doing?' Her voice rose unsteadily and a few people at neighbouring tables glanced over at them curiously. 'Give me my ticket back!'

'All in good time.' Marc pushed his chair away from the table and reached to pick up her luggage. 'Now, let me give you a hand with this.'

'No, thank you!' She tried to stop him, but he was too quick for her and got there first so that her hand just closed over his on the handle. The physical contact made her instantly relinquish the bag and flinch away as if she had been burnt.

He watched as she rubbed at her hand as if trying to erase the memory of his skin against hers.

'Libby…I just want to put things right.' The husky, gentle tone cut straight through her.

'As if you give a damn about that!' She gave him a fulminating glare from vivid blue eyes. 'You are just thinking about a possible PR disaster before your precious client's première.'

Marc shook his head. 'You couldn't be further away from the truth.'

'Well, I don't believe that. In fact I don't believe one word you say any more.' She remained firm and held out her hand. 'Now give me my bag back.'

'No.' The gentle tone was gone now, replaced by a steely kind of calmness that totally infuriated her.

'Look, if you don't give my luggage and my ticket back to me,' she snapped, 'I'm going to start making a scene.'

'Really?' There was a flicker of amusement in his dark eyes now. 'What are you going to do?'

Hell, but this man was infuriating. How she could ever have thought that she loved him! 'I'll…' She cast about frantically in her mind for some threat. 'I'll yell that I've been mugged.'

Marc shrugged. 'Yell away, but I'll just say we are having a lovers' spat, and the French are very understanding about affairs of the heart.'

Before she could say anything to that he was walking away from her, taking her luggage with him. She hesitated for just a second before following him.

'Look, Marc, I can assure you that I have no intentions of talking to the press about my father, so you can just put my bag down, give me my air ticket and let me go.'

'I can't do that,' Marc said tersely.

They were outside now. It had stopped raining, but the roads glistened with water under the street lights. Marc put up his hand and the black limousine that had dropped Libby off pulled up beside them.

Jacques got out and came around to take Libby's bag from Marc and open the doors for them.

'I suppose Jacques told you where I was?' Libby murmured as she watched her bag being deposited in the boot.

'Of course.' Marc nodded towards the car. 'Now, are you going to get in, or am I going to have to put you in there bodily?'

'You wouldn't dare!' She was horrified.

He took a step towards her and she got hurriedly into the car. 'This...this is kidnapping,' she said furiously.

'Don't be so dramatic.' Marc slid in beside her. 'You wanted to see your father and I am making sure you get your wish.'

'I told you, it's too late for that!' Her heart pounded uneasily against her chest.

'No, it's not. I've spoken to Carl and he is waiting for you at his hotel.'

'I've already been to his hotel.' Libby bit down on her lip.

'I know that. But they will let you in now I'm with you.'

Libby shook her head and for a moment her eyes blurred with tears.

'They will, Libby, and I've cleared it with your father. He is expecting you.'

Libby couldn't answer that...couldn't tell him that in fact her father had already seen her...and turned away.

The limousine pulled out onto the busy roads. Libby

sat quietly as far away from Marc on the comfortable long leather seat as she could.

'Would you like a drink?' Marc opened the drinks cabinet opposite. 'I have champagne.'

'I only drink champagne when I have something to celebrate,' Libby said numbly.

'Well, you have got something to celebrate. I'm taking you to see your father.'

Libby shook her head.

'A glass of white wine, then?' Marc reached for a bottle.

'I don't want a drink, Marc. I just want to go back to the airport to catch my plane.'

Marc closed the cabinet and sat back in the seat. 'Look, I am sorry that I told you your father hadn't arrived in France. At the time it seemed like a necessary lie.'

'I bet.' Libby averted her gaze from his. 'You didn't tell me that he was dating his leading lady either.'

'I thought it was your father's place to tell you that. Not mine.'

'But my father didn't want to see me, did he?'

The words dropped into the silence and lay there for what seemed like a never-ending period of time.

'Your father has been under a lot of strain, Libby,' Marc said finally. 'It's not easy being under the full glare of the media spotlight. I know this is difficult for you as well, but I think you should try and cut him some slack.'

Libby looked over at him then, her gaze sharp. 'You should have told me the truth.'

Marc held her gaze steadily. 'I thought about it...but I didn't want to upset you.'

Libby rolled her eyes. 'Oh, please...do you think I am completely naïve?'

'Believe it or not, that is the truth,' he cut across her

firmly. 'Yes, I probably did the wrong thing pretending that your father wasn't here, I realise that now. But I just didn't want to tell you that he wasn't ready to see you.'

This statement truly incensed her. 'He's had twenty years to prepare himself to see me, Marc. Let's not pussy-foot around this any more. The fact is he just doesn't want to see me.'

Marc looked over at her steadily. 'I won't lie to you, Libby. He's very nervous about seeing you, but that is to be expected,' he said quietly.

'Why? Because I've shunned him over the years?' Libby's voice dripped with derision. 'I suppose it was you who leaked that little titbit to the press.'

'I haven't said anything to the press about you, Libby.'

'And I don't believe you.' Her voice trembled with fury.

'Well, it's true.' For a moment his lips slanted in a wry smile. 'If you remember, I'm the one who wanted to keep you out of the press completely. I was all for just issuing a one off statement.'

'Because of course you are *such* a gentleman.' She practically spat the words at him.

He smiled at that, but it was a self-deprecating smile. 'I tried to be.'

Something about the way he looked at her and the husky timbre of his tone cut into her raw emotions.

It was hard to read the expression in his eyes, but she could see a pulse beating in the side of his jaw.

'Libby, I realise I've handled things badly. When I moved you into my house I really did it for the best of intentions. I wanted to help soothe things over between you and your father. I didn't intend for things to go as far as they did between us.' He reached out and touched her face, but she flinched away from him and the rawness inside her became a physical ache.

'But somewhere along the line I—'

'I don't want to hear this. I really mean it.' She steadfastly avoided looking at him. But inside she felt as if her heart were breaking. Those words 'I didn't intend for things to go as far as they did between us' were burning inside her. 'And I don't want to see my father.' The fire had gone from her tone now.

'Libby, I'm not turning back. It's best we get this over with.'

Easy for him to say, she thought. But the idea of facing her father now, knowing he didn't want her here, was too much hurt to bear.

'I don't see the point,' she muttered. 'I just want to go home now.'

'The point is that once you do this you will feel more at peace...be able to move on with your life.' Marc's gentle tone made her heart turn over.

She glared over at him and her eyes shimmered with tears. 'Don't pretend to understand how I feel, Marc... because you have no idea.'

'I think I do,' he said softly.

She shook her head and looked away from him. 'You just think I am cold-hearted and mercenary...fair game, in fact.'

'Libby, I don't think that.'

The warmth and the softness of his tone made her want to cry all the more, but she held herself together with difficulty. 'Don't lie to me, Marc. I know the only reason that you are here now is that you are worried about what I will say to the press about your precious client. You'll protect him to the hilt. You were doing it a while ago with all the spiel about how hard it is for him in the media spotlight.'

'I'm not trying to protect him, Libby; I'm trying to protect you,' he said softly. 'I was trying to explain that Carl is so caught up in his career that he doesn't think clearly sometimes.'

'He was thinking clearly enough a few hours ago when he blanked me in the hotel lobby,' Libby retorted swiftly.

'And he's full of remorse,' Marc said quickly.

'Oh, so you know about that?' Her voice trembled slightly.

'Yes, I got a distraught phone call from him.' Marc's voice was grim. 'You need to see him and sort this out.'

As Marc finished speaking the limousine pulled up outside the Carlton hotel again.

'Do this, Libby, for yourself as much as for him.' Marc's tone was low and persuasive and he reached out and touched her hand. 'It will lay ghosts of the past to rest.'

The touch of his fingers against her skin instantly turned her feelings of anxiety into something much more volatile. She pulled away from him.

'I'll give him five minutes,' she said huskily. 'But then I want to go home, Marc.'

He nodded. 'I'll wait for you in the foyer.'

CHAPTER TWELVE

LIBBY checked her appearance in the mirror outside her father's room. Her hair was sitting in reasonable order, but she smoothed it down further over the bruise at the side of her forehead.

She wished she had stubbornly refused to go through with this. But she was here now, she told herself sensibly, so it was best to get it over with…

With a rapidly beating heart she turned towards the door. At least she was no longer imagining a happy reunion, in fact was under no illusions at all about this meeting…so she didn't know why she felt so nervous.

She knocked firmly on the door.

'Come in, it's open.'

Libby glanced at her watch. Five minutes…then she was out of here, she told herself.

Taking a deep breath, she turned the handle and walked in.

The first thing Libby noticed was how lovely the suite was with panoramic windows looking out over the promenade. Softly shaded lamps lit the room and music was playing in the background.

Then she noticed the man standing in the far shadows of the room.

'Dad?' Her voice was no more than a tentative whisper.

He stepped forward and she could see immediately that it was her father. He was wearing the same dark suit and white shirt that he had been wearing earlier.

But it was the expression on his face that held her riveted. He looked so strained and tense, as if he was as nervous about this meeting as she was.

She couldn't move; she couldn't say anything.

'I'm sorry about…before, Libby. I can hardly believe I did that.' His voice trembled and broke. 'I recognised you straight away, you know.'

'Yes, I realised that.' Her voice was stiff.

'Marc had shown me some photographs of you. But I still would have known it was you, even though you are all grown up and so beautiful. You still look like my daughter… And so like me.'

'Yes, Marc said I was like you…stubborn and a bit difficult, I think were his words.' Libby didn't know why she said that, but it seemed to lighten the atmosphere.

Her dad smiled. 'Marc is a nice guy. He is also a tremendous businessman; I'm lucky to have him. I've given him a difficult time over the last few days.'

'Have you?'

'Oh, yes.' Carl's voice was heavy. 'There was a point when I was so nervous about seeing you that I wasn't even going to come to Cannes for the première. I staged a car accident in the hope of it excusing me. But Marc wouldn't let me away with that; he told me I had to attend the première. He also kept telling me I had to see you, and I kept making excuses…told him I was ill…gave him the run-around.'

'I see.' Libby was surprised, it sounded as if Marc had been batting in her corner all along. But probably for sound business reasons rather than any desire to help her, she told herself quickly. He'd had no compunction about lying to her.

'All you had to do was tell me you didn't want to see me, and I'd have gone away,' she said softly.

Carl frowned. 'It's not that I didn't want to see you,' he said sternly. 'It's not quite that simple.'

'So what was it about?'

Carl shook his head. 'I've let you down, Libby. I know that. And I suppose a lot of what I've done has been done through guilt. Firstly guilt at walking out and secondly guilt at the lies I've told to cover my tracks.'

Abruptly he turned away from her and went across to a sideboard. 'I don't know about you, but I could use a drink. Would you like a whiskey?'

'No, thank you.' She sat down on the arm of one of the chairs.

'I'm sorry I haven't been in touch, Libby.' His voice cracked a little. 'And I'm not talking now about the last few days.'

'No.' She looked down at her shoes. She didn't know what to say.

'I did try.' He turned then and looked at her. 'A year after I left your mother I came back on holiday to England for a few days to see you, but…You were out in the garden with your mum and your stepfather…and you looked like a proper family.' He shrugged. 'You were so young and I had nothing to offer you then…no decent job and no home. It seemed kinder to walk away.'

Libby frowned and glanced up. 'I didn't want anything from you, Dad. I just wanted to see you…even an occasional letter would have been better than nothing!'

Carl's eyes misted with tears. 'I made a bloody mess of everything,' he grated. 'My marriage and my role as a father.'

'You did your best.' Libby didn't know what else to say.

'And it wasn't good enough. I told myself that you were better off without me.' Carl shook his head. 'Your mother and I were very young when we got married, Libby. And, I'll be honest, I found the responsibility hard.'

Libby noticed that his hand was shaking as he took a sip of his drink.

'Dad, I know that the marriage wasn't happy—'

'I told your mother I was leaving. I'd been offered a job in California. Not much of a job, I'll grant you, but I wanted to take it, wanted to pursue my dreams of becoming an actor. She thought we would all go…and I even let her think that for a while…but…' Carl shook his head. 'It wasn't that I didn't love *you*… I just couldn't have afforded to support you both. I needed to be free and it would have been no life for you.'

Libby frowned. 'But I thought Mum left you for Sean?'

Carl shook his head. 'Sean just made things easier for me to leave. At least I knew she had someone and—'

'You mean Mum was with Sean on the rebound?'

Carl shrugged. 'I know he was head over heels in love with her.'

Suddenly everything was becoming clearer in Libby's mind. Her mother must have been so hurt…and it couldn't have been easy being left with a young child. She had made a difficult choice marrying Sean…but she had been lonely and unhappy, had still been in love with Carl, and had known that he wasn't coming back.

No wonder Sean had been so aggressively against her dad, he had probably known her mother had still loved Carl, and had been jealous.

It had been a recipe for disaster.

Carl's voice shook. 'I know I was selfish, Libby, but an opportunity came up for me in California. So I took it, and started over.'

'And you told yourself that I didn't need you any more?' Libby's voice was uneven.

'It was wrong I know that, but I didn't realise what I was throwing away, Libby…and if it's any consolation I have been racked with regret and with guilt ever since.'

'I don't want you to be racked by guilt,' Libby murmured.

'It's probably hard for you to believe, but I never stopped thinking about you. Just before your tenth birthday I sent your mother my address and told her that if you wanted to look me up, I'd love to see you. But you never did get in contact.'

Libby's face drained of colour. 'I didn't get the message,' she said huskily. Then she took a deep breath before admitting, 'And it was just before my tenth birthday that Mum took me to one side and told me you were dead.'

Carl put his glass down on the sideboard and looked at her in horror. 'My God! I didn't think Ellen hated me that much!'

'I don't think she did.' Libby remembered how her mother had looked past her towards Sean as she'd told Libby that lie. 'He's dead,' she had said again.

Libby understood that meaningful tone now. And although she was still appalled by her mother's lie, she could understand it more now. Her mother had wanted to forget the past and make a fresh start with Sean. They had been estranged at the time, but soon after that her stepfather had moved back into the house and things had settled down. The marriage had survived.

'I think she just wanted to protect her marriage.'

'Yes, but to say such a thing!'

'We all make mistakes, Dad, don't we?' she said softly.

'I've made more than my fair share. I've been married three times.'

Libby nodded. 'And now you've met someone else?'

'But this is the real thing, Libby.'

'Well, that's good.' Libby smiled. 'I hope you'll be happy.'

'Thank you,' Carl said emotionally. 'Libby, I have to tell you that I've told a lot of lies where you are concerned. And I feel so ashamed and humbled…but, I mean, how could I tell a man like Marc Clayton that to all intents and purposes I had abandoned my daughter? He's such a decent and honourable kind of bloke and he adores his daughter. He'd never walk away from her. He's a good family man.' Carl shook his head. 'I just couldn't tell him. He would have lost all respect for me.'

'So you told him that you'd tried many times over the years to contact me? Sent me expensive presents?'

Carl's face flushed red with embarrassment.

'It's all right,' Libby told him dryly. 'I'm not particularly bothered what Marc thinks.'

But even as she was saying those words she knew she was lying. She didn't want to care…but she did.

'The lies weren't just for Marc's sake. I didn't want Julia to know what a rubbish father I am either. And I repeated the lies for the press.'

'I thought it was Marc who fed the press those lies,' Libby murmured.

'Marc is too honourable for that.' Carl shook his head. 'I am sorry, Libby. Doing this family-man part in a film has freaked me out a bit; everyone assumes I'm like the character I play. And it's hard to admit I'm not. But I will make things right…if you just give me a few days I will tell everyone the truth.'

Libby shrugged. 'That's up to you. I'm not going to say anything.'

'No, the truth must be told. ' Carl frowned. 'Libby, would you like to come to the première of my film?' he asked suddenly.

'Thanks, Dad, but, you know, I think I've had enough of being in the limelight. I think I'll just go home.'

'Well, maybe you will come and visit me in California.'

'Maybe.'

He crossed the room then and suddenly she found herself enveloped in the warmth of his embrace.

She put her arms up and around his neck and just clung to him. In those few minutes it was as if time went backwards and she was indeed his little girl again…and he was the man she had looked up to and loved with all her heart.

Libby felt a bit emotional when she left the room.

A chapter had closed; she could go home, put all this behind her and get on with her life.

'How did it go?' Marc's deep voice coming from further down the hall made her jump.

'It went OK.' She looked over at him. He looked so handsome…and so concerned that her heart seemed to turn over with a crazy kind of need to run into his arms.

'So what do you want to do now?' He took a step closer.

Hastily she looked away from him. 'Go home, of course.'

'Home to Simon?'

That question made her frown. Simon was the furthest person from her thoughts. 'Does it matter?' she asked softly.

'It matters to me.'

The quietly spoken words made her senses leap. But he

was probably talking about the business of PR, she reminded herself. All he was concerned with was her father's film, and he probably wanted to keep her at his house locked away from the press for as long as possible.

'I've told you I am not going to say anything to the press.' Libby started to search in her bag for a handkerchief, but couldn't find one.

'You're upset!' He reached out and touched her arm. 'Libby, honey, don't cry. I hate seeing you like this.'

'I'm not crying. I'm just a bit emotional after seeing my dad, that's all!' But as she glanced over at him she knew that wasn't all. The fact was, she was in love with Marc Clayton and the thought of leaving here and never seeing him again made her feel as if her heart would truly break into a million tiny pieces.

With difficulty she pulled herself together and glanced at her watch. 'I need to get back to the airport. If I leave now I just might make that flight.'

'I don't think you'll make it.' He said the words softly.

'I have to!' She glared at him through a shimmer of tears.

'No, you don't. You can stay here with me.'

Libby brushed past him towards the lifts. 'Marc, I am not listening to this. I've told you I won't make trouble for Dad's première and I meant it.'

'This isn't about your dad...or the première. This is about us,' Marc said quietly.

'Us?' Her heart lurched crazily and she turned to look at him. 'What do you mean?'

Marc took hold of her hand and led her towards the lifts. 'Let's get out of here.' The doors were open, they stepped inside and Marc pushed the button for the reception.

'Libby, I know you believe that you and Simon can put

our relationship back together, but I don't think he de-
serves a second chance with you. I think…' He paused as
f choosing his words with great care.

'What do you think?' Libby asked curiously.

The lift stopped on the floor beneath and another couple
got in.

Marc put an arm around her shoulder and held her
closer. 'I think it's best we talk privately in the car,' he
murmured against her ear.

Libby felt a shiver of desire shoot through her. His
closeness was intoxicating and, although she tried to tell
herself that trusting anything Marc Clayton said to her was
a big mistake, she couldn't help feel a glimmer of pleasure
at just being near him.

The lift doors slid open on the ground floor and they
stepped out. What did Marc want to say to her? she wondered. Whatever it was she shouldn't listen…she told herself firmly. She should learn by her mistakes of the past.
No man was going to sweet-talk her into things, or take
advantage of her again.

As they left the front entrance of the hotel a bright flash
of lightning lit the sky, followed by an incredibly loud
roar of thunder. And for a moment Libby was glad to
climb inside the waiting limousine. Then Marc got in beside her and the door closed, leaving them alone in the
dark intimacy of the leather interior.

The car pulled out into the traffic.

Marc held her gaze across the limited space between
them and she felt a flutter of apprehension. She leaned
forward a little to talk to the driver. 'Jacques, you will
take me directly to the airport, won't you?'

'He can't hear you through that glass, Libby, and he
can't see you,' Marc told her. 'I've closed the privacy

partition. But don't worry, I've given him his instructions.'

'Oh!' Libby sat back. 'You know, you don't need to come with me to the airport, Marc.' She tried to think sensibly. 'I mean…you have a date with your ex-wife…don't you? Maybe you should keep it.'

'That wasn't a date, Libby; it was dinner to talk about business. Marietta has landed a big part in an epic new film that is being shot over here. They are making a trilogy back to back so it will mean she will be based here in the South of France for at least the next four, maybe five years.'

'Was that what you were talking about when you said that you might be able to live back here in France and have Alice close by?'

'Yes.' He nodded. 'The negotiations are not fully finalised, but it looks like I'm going to get my wish, I'll be back here more or less full time and have my daughter.'

'Congratulations. You must be over the moon.' Libby wondered if Marietta would also be full time in his life again. The thought hurt.

'Yes, life would be pretty near damn perfect except for one thing.'

'What's that?'

'You leaving.'

'Look, Marc, I know you are thinking about my father and his reputation, but I swear I never intended to make any difficulties for him. Really, you can drop this now.'

'I told you, Libby, this has nothing to do with your father. This is to do with you and I.'

Libby stared at him uncertainly.

'I want you to stay,' he said huskily.

'Stay…for the night?'

Marc shook his head. 'Look, I realise you think you

might be in love with this Simon guy, but surely you can sense the chemistry between us? Surely you realise that what we have is too special to throw away?'

Libby was so stunned that she couldn't find her voice.

'I love you, Libby.' Marc leaned forward and took hold of her hands.

'Marc, don't say things like that…even in jest…if you don't mean them,' she whispered unsteadily.

'But I do mean them.' He reached out and stroked the side of her face. 'Forgive me, Libby, but I just can't keep my hands off you. I need you so much it is like a physical ache inside me.'

She stared up at him wordlessly.

'I know I shouldn't have lied about the fact that your father was here; I should have told you he was prevaricating about seeing you. But you looked so damned vulnerable every time we mentioned your dad that I didn't have the heart to tell you he was being difficult…'

'You think I'm a gold-digger,' she accused him numbly. 'You believed all those things my father said about me.'

Marc nodded. 'Yes, I did at first. I just couldn't believe that any man would want to shut his daughter out of his life. And I had no reason not to believe Carl when he said he was heartbroken. And then…'

'And then?' Her eyes held with his and she didn't even dare to breathe.

'And then I met you and all my preconceived ideas were thrown into chaos.'

'You mean you believe me now?' A lone tear trickled down her cheek.

'Oh, darling, please don't cry.' He wiped away the tear with tender fingers and she wondered if this were a dream; maybe at any moment she would wake up. 'Yes, I believe you. As soon as I met you I started to have severe doubts, and then Carl kept making excuses why he couldn't meet with you and I knew then that he wasn't being completely truthful.'

'You didn't say anything.'

'I suppose deep down I was frightened of making a mistake. I don't ever want to go through the heartache I went through with Marietta again...so I thought I'd play things cool.'

'Oh, did you now?'

He nodded. 'And then you marched out of my house and out of my life and I knew I had to say something...even if you reject me, Libby. I can't let you go without saying how I feel. That's why I came after you to the airport tonight.'

'I thought it was because of business...because of my father.'

Marc shook his head. 'I probably don't deserve a second chance, but I'll do anything to win back your trust. Anything. I'm sorry for lying to you about your father, but I promise I did it with the best of intentions.'

The husky words made her heart wrench. 'And you are not in love with Marietta?' she whispered.

He shook his head. 'I'm in love with you,' he said earnestly. 'I think I adored you from the first moment I set eyes on you in that airport.'

'No, you didn't. You thought I was going to make trouble,' she reminded him.

'Will you stop arguing with me?' His voice was gentle. 'Yes, I knew you were going to be trouble...but mainly because I was so damn taken with you.'

'I knew you were going to be trouble as well.' Her voice wobbled precariously.

'Look, Libby, I don't want to take you back to the

airport, but obviously I can't keep you here in France against your will—'

'I suppose you could try,' she said playfully.

'Libby?' He looked at her hopefully. 'And what about Simon?'

'I'm not in love with Simon; I'm in love with you,' she whispered unsteadily.

'Really?' He looked so worried, so earnestly solemn, that she half smiled.

'Marc, nobody has ever made me feel the way you do. I'm wild about you. Why else do you think I've responded to you the way I have…made love to you the way I have?' She shook her head. 'I know I tried to pretend that I was a modern woman and it didn't mean anything. But I was lying. It meant so much that I was crazy with longing and love for you. And I realised that Simon was never right for me. I never felt like this about him—'

Then suddenly they were kissing. It was a deeply passionate embrace and it shook Libby so intensely that she could only cling to him in wonder.

'I thought you said you didn't mean for things to go this far between us,' she reminded him breathlessly as he pulled back.

'And I didn't,' he whispered. 'I never meant to let my heart get so involved, but the short time I have spent with you has changed my life around,' he murmured huskily. 'Since my divorce I've kept relationships at a distance, not wanted any commitments, and then you waltz in with your big blue eyes and your warm, loving ways and I was hooked, completely captivated.'

'Were you?' She looked up at him wondrously.

'You have no idea the control it took to try and keep my hands off you.'

'You mean you were exercising some control?' Libby half smiled at him.

'Yes…' Marc smirked at her. 'But I knew that I had well and truly lost any battle on that score.' He pulled her closer in against his chest.

'Marc, I love you with all my heart,' she said quietly.

It was a long time before either of them spoke again. Their kisses were passionate and their caresses more and more heated.

'You'd better tell Jacques not to go to the airport,' Libby said as she snuggled closer.

'Jacques isn't going to the airport. He's taking us home.'

'Marc!' She pulled back and looked at him in mock horror. 'Isn't that called taking me for granted?'

'I don't give up without a fight, Libby.' He pulled her back. 'I knew once I'd got you back to my place that the chemistry would take over and you'd see sense.'

'I was never going to get back with Simon, you know.' Libby bit down on her lip. 'Not only did he finish with me, but he ran up a load of debts on my credit card when he left.'

Marc pulled back from her with a frown. 'Why didn't you tell me that?'

'You already thought I was a no good gold-digger. I don't think telling you that would have helped.' She leaned against him and sighed. 'Besides, I had my pride.'

'I'm sorry that I doubted you, Libby.'

'So you should be.' She smiled and reached to kiss him.

'So if you've forgiven me, does that mean you'll marry me?'

For a moment Libby thought she had misheard him. She pulled away and looked at him in surprise. 'Are you serious?'

'I would never joke about something as serious as this.'
His eyes were gentle and watchful.

When she didn't answer him immediately he reached
out to her.

'I'm so much in love with you that it hurts, and the
answer is, yes, I'd love to marry you.'

Marc kissed her then with such sweet, overwhelming
passion that she melted in against him with pleasure.

She loved the strength of his body against hers, the feel
of his lips pressed against hers, but most of all she loved
the feeling of truly belonging. It was as if this was the
place where she was meant to be... No matter what happened in the outside world, this was what mattered. This
was where she was cherished and protected and loved.
This at last was the real thing.

MILLS & BOON®   1205/01b

Live the emotion

Modern
romance™

A RUTHLESS AGREEMENT by Helen Brooks

Lawyer Zeke Russell *always* wins. So when his ex-fiancée
Melody Taylor asks for help, he takes the chance to settle
an old score! Melody has no choice but to swallow
her pride and accept his proposition: rekindle their
relationship – though this time it's on *his* terms...

THE CARIDES PREGNANCY by Kim Lawrence

Naïve Becca Summer doesn't set out to be seduced by
Greek tycoon Christos Carides – but, with no love lost
between their families, he conceals his identity and she
falls into his bed! She longs to forget the bittersweet
memories of their lovemaking, but she's expecting
Christos's child...

PRINCE'S LOVE-CHILD by Carole Mortimer

Five years ago Sapphie Benedict lost her virginity to hunky
Hollywood screenwriter Rik Prince. But, thinking he
was in love with her sister, she left and didn't tell him of
the consequence of their affair! Now Sapphie meets Rik
again, and realises she has never stopped loving him. But
their lives are more complicated than ever...

MISTRESS ON DEMAND by Maggie Cox

Rich and irresistible, Dominic van Straten lived in a
different world from Sophie's. Even after their reckless,
hot encounter, she felt it best to go back to her ordinary
life. But Dominic wasn't about to let her go – he wanted
her as his full-time social hostess, travel partner and live-
in lover...

On sale 6th January 2006

*Available at most branches of WHSmith, Tesco, ASDA,
Borders, Eason, Sainsbury's and most bookshops*

Visit www.millsandboon.co.uk

Reality TV,
real love...and no commercials...

Surviving Sarah *by Vicki Lewis Thompson*
Luke Richards has entered a battle-of-the-brawn reality
TV show for one reason: he wants the "prize" —
Sarah Donovan!

The Great Chase *by Julie Elizabeth Leto*
When rival private investigators Charlotte and Sam partner
for a cross-country reality show, Charlotte can't help
wondering if working together might not be a lot more
fun after all.

The Last Virgin *by Jennifer LaBrecque*
Andrea signs up for a singles show and discovers her
virginity is up for grabs. Contestant Zach is determined to
prove reality TV isn't real at all, but he doesn't count on
wanting to claim the winner's prize so much!

On sale 6th January 2006

Available at most branches of WHSmith, Tesco,
ASDA, Borders, Eason, Sainsbury's and most bookshops

Visit our website at www.millsandboon.co.uk

FREE!

4 Books
and a surprise gift!

We would like to take this opportunity to thank you for reading this Mills & Boon® book by offering you the chance to take FOUR more specially selected titles from the Modern Romance™ series absolutely FREE! We're also making this offer to introduce you to the benefits of the Reader Service™—

- ★ **FREE home delivery**
- ★ **FREE gifts and competitions**
- ★ **FREE monthly Newsletter**
- ★ **Exclusive Reader Service offers**
- ★ **Books available before they're in the shops**

Accepting these FREE books and gift places you under no obligation to buy, you may cancel at any time, even after receiving your free shipment. Simply complete your details below and return the entire page to the address below. You don't even need a stamp!

YES! Please send me 4 free Modern Romance books and a surprise gift. I understand that unless you hear from me, I will receive 6 superb new titles every month for just £2.75 each, postage and packing free. I am under no obligation to purchase any books and may cancel my subscription at any time. The free books and gift will be mine to keep in any case.

P5ZEF

Ms/Mrs/Miss/Mr ....Initials.................................

                                                                                    BLOCK CAPITALS PLEASE

Surname ....

Address..

....

....Postcode ....

Send this whole page to:
UK: FREEPOST CN81, Croydon, CR9 3WZ